The Nativity Stories

"And they shall call His name Immanuel"
Matthew 1:23

B. MICHAEL FEE

authorHOUSE®

AuthorHouse™
1663 Liberty Drive
Bloomington, IN 47403
www.authorhouse.com
Phone: 1 (800) 839-8640

Published by AuthorHouse 10/27/2015

ISBN: 978-1-5049-5852-3 (sc)
ISBN: 978-1-5049-5853-0 (e)

Print information available on the last page.

This book is printed on acid-free paper.

Dedicated

Andrew J. Barbaro
1975-2009

Andrew C. Hall
1964-2012

Daniel A. Nikas
1976-2011

"Earth has no sorrow that Heaven cannot heal"
Thomas Moore

Dedication Salutation

The young men to whom this work is dedicated, were men of extraordinary courage, charity, and love of family. That they lived, known by me, by the circle of relatives and friends I love and admire, makes these few words all the harder and more important to write.

C. S. Lewis, the peerless Christian apologist from England, wrote, after losing his wife to cancer,

"I suppose that if one were forbidden all salt one wouldn't notice it much more in any one food than in another. Eating in general would be different, every day, at every meal. It is like that. The act of living is different all through. Her absence is like the sky, spread over everything."

A Grief Observed

For these families, children, spouses and partners, siblings, parents, and friends, traumatized with unanswered questions and thoughts of what might have been, are left indeed as Lewis himself describes: 'their absence is like the sky, spread over everything'. For myself, I can only speak of them as a group, young men ripening in their duties as fathers, struggling within the intense cultural obstacles pressing down relentlessly on young families and relationships and yet, persevering. I remember them all with a smile one moment and a tear the next, knowing, that all those who knew and loved them are marked for the rest of their lives, with this same mixture of joy and sadness. And at the moment when it mattered most, for each and every one of them, the armory of detection and restorative therapies offered by modern medicine, utterly failed them… falling just beyond their reach and refuge. The end of this little book, points to a different moment, a different "sky, spread over everything"… a moment when another young man, centuries ago, died so that we might live, so that we might be healed.

Andy, Andrew, and Dan, all interacted with this other moment, this other man. They questioned Him, they talked to Him. He was with them more than they knew. And may He now bless them and keep them in His loving embrace for all time.

Contents

Foreword

For centuries, Jewish and Christian scholars, historians, archeologists, etc. have attempted to "flesh out" in finer detail, the recorded accounts of the four evangelists. They have been constrained by both time and the Gospels themselves. We remain, to this day, as unfamiliar as we have ever been of the fuller knowledge regarding the most important figures written of in these testaments. Yes we have real locations, yes we have real historical persons, who can be and have been validated as to time and place... but there is more, much more. A casual mention of a name and little else, yet the story behind story is unknown.

As a fiction writer, there are but few constraints (unlike scholars and historians), that one need abide by way of guidance or accuracy, save for scripture itself. In this case, I attempt to plant my mind and feet on the straight path, and hopefully, in a most respectful and honorable manner, utilize the time tested Hebrew practice of midrash, as I hold these characters up to the light, turning them in unusual ways, catching something that may or may not have been there, but rings true to this believer's ears.

My hope is that upon reading these stories, you and yours will set your minds free to wander about in these, the most extraordinary of human times.

B. Michael Fee

Nazareth

Many of those who lived in Nazareth believed the town was given its name from a derivation the old Hebrew word for branch, *ne-ser*, and from it would spring the fulfillment of the prophecy from Isaiah 11: 1-10,

"And there shall come forth a rod out of the stem of Jesse, and a Branch shall grow out of his roots: And the spirit of the LORD shall rest upon him, the spirit of wisdom and understanding, the spirit of counsel and might, the spirit of knowledge and of the fear of the LORD; And shall make him of quick understanding in the fear of the LORD: and he shall not judge after the sight of his eyes, neither reprove after the hearing of his ears: But with righteousness shall he judge the poor, and reprove with equity for the meek of the earth: and he shall smite the earth with the rod of his mouth, and with the breath of his lips shall he slay the wicked. And righteousness shall be the girdle of his loins, and faithfulness the girdle of his reins. The wolf also shall dwell with the lamb, and the leopard shall lie down with the kid; and the calf and the young lion and the fatling together;

and a little child shall lead them. And the cow and the bear shall feed; their young ones shall lie down together: and the lion shall eat straw like the ox. And the sucking child shall play on the hole of the asp, and the weaned child shall put his hand on the cockatrice' den. They shall not hurt nor destroy in all My holy mountain: for the earth shall be full of the knowledge of the LORD, as the waters cover the sea. And in that day there shall be a root of Jesse, which shall stand for an ensign of the people; to it shall the Gentiles seek: and his rest shall be glorious."

The local Rabbi, whose synagogue sat nearly atop the highest hill of the town, began every service with this reminder to the people… it would be from ***here*** that Yahweh would raise up His people… a stem, a holy root… wisdom and righteousness… the world as they knew it would change forever.

Nazareth was a commoner's town, there were no rich Jews here… it was dusty… the roads, 2 of them, from the hills to the flatland, where the town well stood, converged there, and kept going all the way to Sepphoris, about 4 miles away to the north. Sepphoris gave many tradesmen in Nazareth year-round work as it harbored numerous Roman building projects and repair operations. It was also a city of some wealth, and barracked many Roman soldiers, and Herod's troops.

Joseph was one who traveled to Sepphoris. The tradesmen always moved along that road together… for there were highway bandits in the hills they passed, but if they walked as a group, they were always avoided. Tradesmen were strong, and able to defend, punish any attackers. This was especially true of Joseph.. He was bigger and stronger than anyone else… and he had his red sandalwood staff… a formidable weapon which he knew how to use. Bandits kept their distance when Joseph was present… several had made an early mistake, and paid dearly for it, and word had spread. They would let Joseph be… and anyone who traveled with him.

The Messenger

Gabriel, a most honored and heavenly being, referred to as archangel, one of the angels who "stand before God" received from the Most High, the greatest of all tasks... the announcement of the most important of all human events, the birth of the Immanuel. He is acclaimed multiple times in Scripture... most notably in this series of events, sent as the messenger to Zechariah, who questioned his authenticity and belief in what was being revealed, and was struck mute for his lack of faith... and Mary, the virgin mother of the Christ, who did believe and desires to fulfill the will of God in her life.

Zechariah, a priest of the Abijah, of the descendants of Aaron, and husband of Elizabeth, of the tribe of Judah, in a time honored and required element of Temple worship in Jerusalem, stood alone, as worship demanded... he stood not within the Holy of Holies, for he was not a high priest, but he began the ceremony in the burning of incense to the Lord. Zechariah had waited all his priestly life for this moment... to come into "the Holy Place", as the lone representative of the Jewish nation, while the people, prayed intently, outside the Temple.

He was nearing the end of the exacting protocol, when suddenly, a voice broke through the absolute silence and candlelight darkness… "Do not be afraid, Zechariah"… Zechariah, startled, rose up from his prostrate position… he slowly turned to view into the darkness… but despite the words, he ***was*** afraid… and wondered how this person, he gave no mind to anything other than that, how could this person have slipped by the Temple guards?

The voice spoke again, "Your prayer is heard by the Most High, and your wife, Elizabeth will bear you a son, and you shall call his name John. And you will have joy and gladness, and many will rejoice at his birth; for he will be great before the Lord, and he shall drink no wine nor strong drink, and he will be filled with the Holy Spirit, even from his mother's womb. And he will turn many sons of Israel to the Lord their God, and he will go before him in the spirit and power of Elijah, to turn the hearts of the fathers to the children, and the disobedient to the wisdom of the just, to make ready for the Lord a people prepared."

Zechariah continued to peer into the darkness… "Who is this speaking to me?" he thought. "None of the priests ever mentioned visions or voices doing this… what is the matter with me?"

Then Zechariah's eyes were opened to the figure… not a man… but something out of history… a creature… not of this world… Zechariah, had seen drawings, and heard descriptions of angels… he had no doubt that who had been speaking and revealing to him was none other than Gabriel, the angel of judgment… but even with this, he questioned in his mind what he was being told… his doubt was deep, and he questioned even his eyes and ears… even here, the Lord's house… and the incense continued to burn, giving an other worldly sense to the place.

"How shall I know this?" said Zechariah to the figure… "for I am an old man, and my wife is advanced in years."

Then, the angel, now fully revealed in all his splendor and glory before him, spoke to him in rebuke...

"I am Gabriel, who stand in the presence of God; and I was sent to speak to you, and to bring you this good news. And behold, you will be silent and unable to speak until that day that these things come to pass, because you did ***not*** believe my words, which will be fulfilled in their time."

When Zechariah, trembling and unsteady, emerged from the Temple, the people saw he was changed dramatically and could not speak but tried to communicate what had happened in the Holy Place… it was a long time before he was able to go home. His experience had caused a firestorm of activity and arguments in the Temple courtyards… and beyond.

And lo, what the angel had said to him came to pass in a few days. Elizabeth conceived. A joy beyond anything she had experienced in her life. God had lifted the burden of barrenness and her dishonor before men. She, who did believe, as her husband had written it all down, would bear a son.

Mary

It was warm that morning… unusually so. This was the ending of winter but by mid-day the temperature grew until it was passed 96 degrees Fahrenheit. And there was an unusual fragrance in the air. Hyacinths. But this was not *their* season either… and the scent grew stronger as the day broke, giving the entire town of Nazareth the flavor of spring before its time. There were actually civil conversations and feelings of goodwill all throughout the marketplace… another uncommon occurrence.

Mary was with her mother, Anne, as they purchased figs and small loaves of bread. Anne was a particularly revered member of the Nazarene community… for she had "spoken with angels".

Before she knew she had conceived, it was said an angel came to her and revealed she would have a daughter… and that the child would be special in the eyes of Yahweh… holy and pure... beloved. She would be called Mary.

And it came to pass as was foretold. This story filtered through Nazareth, from Hebrew house to Hebrew house, and as Mary grew, it was clear to all, that she was indeed, precious in the eyes of the Lord.

"Anne, my sister, how are you feeling this day?" said a woman from a neighboring house as she shopped… "and this wonderful bouquet?" she threw her hand twirling in the air… "it reminds you of a wedding, eh?… but no one is marrying in Nazareth today. Strange, don't you think?" Anne smiled and said, "the Lord gives us a present today, does He not?" The woman nodded and started good-natured haggling with the herb seller.

"I think we are finished here, Mary… weariness grows on me more and more it seems."

"Yes, mother… let me carry the packages… you can lean on my elbow as we walk." So they moved, slowly and deliberately, taking a sit down about halfway. "Did you see Joseph working at the window down the street from the market, Mary?"

"Yes mother, I saw him."

"I don't think he noticed us among the crowd…

he was intent on his work as always… so honest in his days' work, Mary… a good man, righteous and patient… a good husband." Anne was as sure of this as anything in her life… "God has chosen ***him***." She whispered to herself.

"Yes mother, I believe he will be." Mary was betrothed to Joseph, blessed by the local elders and Rabbi. It had been 4 weeks now… according custom, Joseph and Mary could live together during the betrothal period, but Joseph thought it best, for lots of reasons, that she continue to live at her birth home.

"The time would come soon enough" he had reasoned.

Exhaustion slowly crept over everyone and everything as the day continued to unfold. Mary and her parents stayed inside their darkened home for the rest of it to stay cool. The heat was relentless. She was just cleaning the evening bowls when her mother called from the roof. Jews in Nazareth, as well as other places, often went to their flat, short-walled roofs in the summer evenings to sleep in the cool breezes of the Mediterranean… and this day was just like summer.

But this was not why Anne was calling Mary.

"Mary, you must come up… your father and I… everyone in town is on the rooftops. It's the sunset, Mary… it's glorious. Joachim is praising Adonai for such a beautiful gift… everyone is."

"What a strange day this has been" Anne was thinking,

"the feel to it is different… a gentleness somehow" and shook her head thoughtfully… but she *said* none of this.

Mary gathered her sleeping mat and blanket and ran up the stairs to the roof. As soon as she saw it, she too fell upon her knees. Anne and Joachim were already praising at their sleeping places at the back of the roof, quenched in the cooling breezes, refreshed from the heat.

The sun was enormous as it hovered over the endless Mediterranean horizon… and of a very rare color indeed… the sun was a blood-apricot.

The bouquet of hyacinths was now laced with lily and rosemary… rapidly filling the night air. Mary's heart was suddenly beating madly in her chest. She rose and walked to the corner of the roof, her soft black hair fingered in the gentle wind.

Virtually all of Nazareth was visible to her there… the shops, the homes, the animals, the families, even the

Rabbi, who was on *his* roof, could be seen… and slowly, as if overpowered by an ocean wave, they **all** settled where they were, falling into deep sleep… foundering down, yielding to this strange repose. House after house, the families lay down peacefully in unexplained, mystic slumber. Even Joseph, who had turned away from the sunset to look in her direction, was relenting to the unexplainable event.

All Nazarenes were… all, that is, except Mary. She remained focused on the dynamic sun, now changing color, even while the aromas intensified… "it all seems to be connected", she was thinking… her body wobbled slightly as she attempted a step forward, yet did not move. Mesmerized by the now accelerating intermix of colors which she could not understand, she closed her eyes for a long moment… but the colors seemed equally as strong on the "inside" as on the outside… she was amazed. She breathed deeply. Her heart settled too, into a slow, deliberate rhythm… quite the opposite of moments ago… it was a serenity… as if the colors, like the fragrances affecting the town, were tenderly swooning her.

She could feel herself, lifting off the roof, but she had no sense of panic… this too had never happened… not even the "magicians" coming through during festival could do this.

She remained there. Suspended in one place… inches from the rooftop but not touching it. Hovering like the doves which Joachim bred.

In an instant it seemed, the sun was streaming every color she had ever seen, straight toward her.

She held out her arms as the glow and hues reached and swirled around her. A luminous tornado of impossible gradations of color swallowed her up. The richness of the tapestry grew and grew. There was nothing now but color… everywhere. She could see no buildings, no ocean, no trees or roads. Nothing existed for her now except the brilliance swirling around her.

And she was neither warm nor cold, an almost perfect temperature… "like being in the womb of God" she thought.

As the vibrancy roiled ever more and more beautiful, she became aware of a presence… just beyond the orbiting fresco. The colors shrouded the presence but did not obscure it.

Unlike anything she had ever seen… larger than a man, but not like a man… something else. It bowed to her and she saw what she thought were tightly folded wings down it's back. And it was white, like the marble floors in Jerusalem. Then, raising its head, it spoke:

"Hail, Full of Grace."

This was by no means a customary greeting… this was a holy salutation. She had never heard it before addressed to a woman… but pondered it as the creature continued to bow.

"The Lord is with you, Mary. Do not be afraid, for you have found great favor with the Almighty God."

And with these words, Mary's eyes were opened.

"I am Gabriel, Messenger from the Heavenly Kingdom. I have been sent to show you your people… your history… and to prepare you." And with those words, a portal opened in the storm of swirls and streaks. It was about the size and shape of the well mouth in the center of Nazareth.

"Mary, see what the Lord God reveals to you…" and with that, scenes of old came into view… at first they were things she did not understand… blinding light hurdling everywhere at once… objects speeding in every direction… then water… then land, with flowers and trees with fruit.

Then animals, strange and beautiful… birds, fish. And in an instant, the beauty and the peacefulness ceased… shattered in the crackling of lightning and dark and hissing… a naked man and woman running… the wind howling as in pain.

The portal surged as she watched men fight and kill each other. And the sound, the hissing, rising and falling.

The portal changed then, as if closing and re-opening its mouth. The scene was one of water and wind.

An enormous covered boat was being tossed about in a wild and raging sea far in the distance, with rain and wind pounding it in a grey and angry storm.

The name Noah passed through her mind. She remembered the story… now, she experienced it. The boat vanished as something else came into view.

Suddenly, a man was in front of her, older than Joachim, her father. He was half-sitting in profile with a huge heavy fire pot ***moving***, on its own, just above the ground, between two rows of things. She could not recognize what they were in the dark. "What am I seeing", she thought?... "how does something move above the ground like it is walking without legs?" Mary could make nothing of it.

She heard a voice then, a voice of power. The voice seemed to come from everywhere… clear and deep.

The voice promised the man much land and many descendants… and a new name: Abraham.

Then she remembered. Abram was given a new name by the Almighty God himself.

Yes, Abraham, Father of the Jewish Nation.

The commanding voice also called that all males be henceforth circumcised as a sign of their covenant with

Him. Abraham nodded. It was the beginning of the brit milah.

More scenes passed before Mary; the stories she had been taught since her youth, and the visions she was encountering all began to align in her mind… armies, victories, defeats… betrayals… and finally, Joseph, son of Jacob (Israel), one of the twelve brothers, sold into slavery and brought to Egypt where the Lord watches over him and elevates him within the house of Pharaoh.

Many generations later, with the descendants and re-united families of Jacob living in Egypt, in the land of Goshen, Egypt enslaves the Jewish people. And so God raises up Moses to deliver His people from their oppression.

Mary loved Moses, as all the Jewish people did… and now she was seeing him as he really was, strong, persistent, a man who encountered the Almighty in the bush which burned but was not consumed… and giving himself, prostrate on the ground to the task God had created him for… deliver His people from the Egyptians.

Mary witnessed it all.

The pillar of fire, the wandering in the desert, the manna, the golden calf, the Ten Commandments given on Mt. Sinai. She watched also, as the Lord's prophets continually chastened the people as they strayed and worshipped false idols. She saw Daniel, a favorite of hers, in the den of lions… and Shadrach, Meshach and Abednego, who were thrown into the fiery furnace of Nebuchadnezzar and emerged, when called by him, completely unharmed.

And so it went on like this for a long time, Jewish men and women of history who did not fall and worship false idols, brought before Mary for her to see. Mary would come to realize that the entire Torah, the Old Testament of Judaism was pointing toward her coming Son, the Savior, the Messiah. And after all was completed in His life, He would give it up for the sins of the people… and rise on the third day… the first day of the new creation. And it would be on this day, as two of His disciples traveled *away* from Jerusalem, toward a Roman garrison town called Emmaus, that Yeshua Himself would intercept them and "open their minds" to the scriptures, setting their hearts on fire, and ultimately turning them around to head back to Jerusalem. Mary's mind was "opened" by Yahweh, using the portal, revealing and preparing her.

And then the portal closed. All was eerily quiet in Nazareth. Almost without breath.

She could feel the embrace of eternal color flooding through her, and her heart burned with truth within her… the Messenger spoke again:

"Mary… blessed are you to see what no man has seen. The Almighty has delivered His people from their oppressors, from their slavery. He has kept His covenant with them… now He will deliver them again… this time, and forever, from their sins…

Behold, you will conceive in your womb and bear a son, and you shall call his name Yeshua.

He will be great, and will be called the Son of the Most High; and the Lord God will give to him the throne of David, and he will reign over the house of Jacob forever; and of his kingdom there will be no end."

Mary marveled at the Messenger's words. She would bear a son… but how?... she had not known her betrothed, Joseph… and tried to think this out in her mind. Gabriel seemed to know this and said:

"The Holy Spirit will come upon you, and the power of the Most High will overshadow you;

Therefore the child to be born will be called holy, the Son of God."

And with that, the colors changed to a brilliance never before seen… a white-ness unlike any other… and a sound like the rush of a mighty wind consumed her, pitching her back. As she closed her eyes, she said: "Behold, I am the handmaid of the Lord, let it be to me according to your word"… and remembered nothing more.

In another part of the ancient world… far, far to the east, in Persia, a middle-aged man… a merchant, astronomer, philosopher, and counsel to the King, was intently watching the night skies. Balthazar of Susa, at the base of the magnificent Zagros Mountains had read the Hebrew texts and had been visited in a dream. The event foretold was about to take place… the event that would change the world. It would be heralded by a new celestial body, a star of great light… and as he surveyed, the sky darkened… and there, emerging above the mountains, was something brilliant, new and never before seen. And this heavenly body would lead him, and two important friends, to the newborn king… the Savior of the world.

Joseph

Joseph bar Jacob had lived his entire life in the little town of Nazareth. He was a direct descendant of David… the hero, sinner and king, many generations before.

Joseph, born to parents Jacob and Hannah was a quiet boy… but strong of body and mind. His scholarship as a child in learning the Torah, and then the Books of the Prophets and The Book of Psalms singled him out at synagogue from his peers… yet all were inexplicably drawn to him… this strong and humble child. He was a natural leader… and never allowed any of the other children to bully or be bullied in his age group. The local Rabbi too sensed something special about him and occasionally tutored him privately… perhaps hoping Joseph would "take his yoke" at a time when he was of age.

Joseph bar Jacob was a model of obedience at home as well as in synagogue. Taking on chores without being asked, and leavening the burden on his father, Jacob, who labored as a potter and clay vessel maker. Joseph learned this trade quite young, and worked the clay well… but he was genuinely gifted working with wood and carpenter tools.

It just seemed to flow so easily out of him. His mother's brother, was a master carpenter now, and Joseph spent many free hours in his shop learning the different woods, the grains, the softness and hardness. He also was a natural with the tools, practicing on leftover woods from completed jobs. His uncle would take him, as he got older, to worksites, mostly in Sepphoris, the nearest big city, which was always being expanded and built up by Herod the First. It was about an hour's walk, which gave Joseph plenty of time to ask questions of his uncle, Ephron, about his skills.

Ephron was patient with Joseph, and quite pleased to see his nephew so eager to learn.

And Joseph saw other things in Sepphoris. It was a Hellenistic city. Gentiles. All the idols and cruelty of the soldiers toward the poor. Ephron saw it too, and shielded Joseph as best he could from the debauchery that bred there.

"We give an honest day of work, and then we go home." Ephron would say..."the rest, our God will deal with." Joseph listened quietly, and remembered... especially the poor and the widows... who were often treated with contempt. He recalled the Psalmist, in Psalm 58, where their God expresses Himself, through the Psalmist, as Father...

> "Father of orphans, defender of widows,
> Such is God in his holy dwelling;
> God gives the lonely a permanent home,
> makes prisoners happy by setting them free,
> but rebels must live in an arid land."

This Psalm, which stood out in the mind of Joseph all his life, would eventually, bring both Joseph and Mary together…

Any earnings Joseph realized on these working trips with Ephron and others from the shop, were always given to the family, and the faith. And, as time passed, Joseph bar Jacob grew into a man of uncommon height and strength for a Nazarene. His shoulders, broad and thick, muscled heavily from lifting the heavy loads in the woodshop since his youth. Hands, rough and powerful… forearms and biceps fully developed rivaling any soldier or Centurion. And when he reached an age, every evening, save the Sabbath and feast days, he would walk into the hills. The quiet there… the time with God.

Joseph could see, as he reached the very top of the hills, to the north, the areas of Zebulon and Naphtali, the mountains and the snow-covered Mt. Hermon, which marked for him the lands of Lebanon, province of Syria. Looking to the sun setting in the west, he could see the coast of Tyre and the sparkling blue Mediterranean.

Again looking west, the rising Mount Carmel where the prophet Elijah struggled with the 450 "prophets" of Baal and the 400 "prophets" of Asherah… and defeated them. Joseph remembered this from the teachings in the synagogue, and the Book of Kings... then he looked south. It was there, the continuing road, constantly traveled by pilgrims, to Jerusalem… and beyond, to Egypt. He did not know it yet, nor did any of them, that a census of the people was under design by Rome… and that each (man) would travel to the place of his birth… for Joseph bar Jacob, this meant going to Bethlehem… a trip of nearly 80 miles.

He would take his staff, his prized red sandalwood, which was thick and strong, a staff he had worked on for years… a gift, raw and unformed, from his uncle Ephron, (leftover from a special project for the King). Joseph spent many, many hours shaping and smoothing it… Ephron counseling him as he went…"and keep it at a man's height, my height for example, for you will have this many years… it is rock hard, and, when oiled, will never rot… it is a real treasure, Joseph, we do not see many woods like it… all imported for the palace in Sepphoris… this single piece, unused."

And it all just flowed out of Joseph without thinking… the red sandalwood, the red (albeit faded) outer garment he wore when he went to synagogue or his walks into the high country… for red, like blood, like the Sardius Stone upon which the name of Judah was inscribed, was all part of his life. The tribes of Israel could distinguish one another in various ways, one way was the color of the outer garment. Joseph would wear this covering when he returned to Bethlehem when the time came.

Joseph bar Jacob was "taken aside" by the Rabbi of Nazareth and the Elders of the synagogue to meditate on a betrothal to Mary ben Joachim, whom they considered in very high regard, and wanted, what they collectively agreed was the best match of an eligible son and an eligible daughter in the town. And they wanted this announcement before any other interfering parties might take action. "The Lord simply has made you two for each other… that is our collective judgment."

Joseph listened, seated in synagogue in silence. It was true, he said, that Mary ben Joachim was a holy and worthy woman, a virgin and knowledgeable in the Torah, more so than many others her age. He would be inclined to this betrothal, but would pray on the matter. Mary had caught his eye more than once, he said

He left, and as it was growing near the end of the day, he took his staff and walked to the highest point in the town. He stayed and prayed for hours. Going over the Psalms in his mind, the history of Israel, the Roman occupation, the influence of Greek culture and worshipping of idols… and the rule of Herod the Great… a plague sent upon the people. The time was ripe, as it was forming in his mind, for the Messiah, promised of old, one who would deliver the people of God.

Amidst all these thoughts and prayers, the face of Mary kept appearing to him.

"What does this mean?" he pondered. He felt a surge of wind, blowing right through him, sweeping out his mind… but Mary remained.

Joseph returned to the Rabbi the next morning and told him he would have an answer for him by the next Sabbath. That very evening, Joseph hurried from the shop early and stopping home, picked up the extra-large clay water vessel (with cover), which he had commissioned his father to craft and proceeded to the town well to fill it with water. When full, it would weigh over 100 pounds… which Joseph could easily carry. He filled it, put the lid in place, and walked, carrying the filled vessel to the widow Silla's home. He placed it at the front entrance and spoke in a voice which could be heard inside, "Shalom, Silla ben Jonah… it is Joseph bar Jacob with a present…"

Voices could be heard coming to the entrance… Joseph waited.

"Shalom Joseph, and what is this?"… Silla was astonished.

"A new clay water vessel, extra-large, fashioned by my father… I give it to you, and will place it where you wish as it is quite heavy with the water."

"Oh Joseph bar Jacob, you are so kind to this old woman… please follow me"… so in they went to the kitchen area.

"Here, Joseph, this is a good place… where I will always see it and remember… it is so beautiful."

As Joseph placed it down, he noticed another woman, a young woman, with her head bowed to the ground. Silla spoke to him. "Joseph, do you know Mary ben Joachim?... I know you have seen her at the synagogue with the other women… she, like you, remembers the widows and orphans in Nazareth… she has brought me four loaves of bread."

"Shalom, Mary ben Joachim… you are very kind to do this for Silla. May the Lord's blessing be upon you and your family." Mary nodded but out of deference and respect to this man, did not look up. Joseph turned and asked Silla if she required anything repaired (he was hoping she would say yes so he could stay longer in Mary's presence), but Silla replied all was well… nothing needed and thanked him profusely. As he went to the entrance he looked back… this time, Mary too was looking… they locked eyes for what seemed like eternity, and then she looked demurely down again.

Silla was widowed when her husband, travelling alone to Jerusalem attending to a small but urgent legal matter, was set upon by thieves and highwaymen, and killed after being robbed.

This was several years ago now, and Joseph and his family, and Mary and her family, and others too… now looked in and cared for Silla, as she had had no children… and lived alone.

Per usual, the next day, Joseph began his day with prayer, and noticed an unusual fragrance permeating the air… his parents remarked on it too. As he left, with his tools, to go down beyond the market to do some repair work with Ephron, he heard women speaking of the pleasant sweetness in the town… "like a wedding…" is what he heard more than once. Meeting his uncle Ephron, he asked whether someone was getting married today or not… Ephron did not know, but it was the wrong season for hyacinth… which is what the bouquet resembled… "ah, but it is wonderful is it not?" Joseph agreed that it was indeed.

It was later that morning that Mary and her mother, Anne, had noticed Joseph, rebuilding a window in a building further away from the market. Mary watched him for a very long time… always swinging on the side of the market stalls so she could see him working.

The day wore on… the temperature soared, and the people all gathered on their roofs to escape the heat and sleep in the cooling Mediterranean breezes. Joseph and his parents and aunt who lived with them were no different. At near sunset, people started gathering... waving and bidding "Shalom" across the spans between homes.

But they all, as if by beckoning, marveled and stood captivated, by the extraordinary sunset this night... and the overpowering bouquet of flowers and spices wafting on the gentle wind.

Mary stood near the edge of the summit of her house looking for the house of Joseph and his parents... they were several sections away on another road leading down and away... but she found it... and to her amazement, Joseph was turned away from the sunset, looking at her. He raised his hand in greeting, and she hers, as the sky darkened, and the sun began its miracle.

The last thing Joseph remembered as he lay down overcome with sleep, was the white light swirling around Mary... and he knew no more.

Hebron

Early the following day, from the miracle which Joseph witnessed that had enveloped Mary, he went directly to the Rabbi and confirmed his acceptance of what the Rabbi and the Elders had suggested… that he accept Mary as his wife. The Jewish custom of betrothal sometimes varied slightly from tribe to tribe, even town to town, but in Nazareth, both families were involved, with the woman, the bride-to-be, given the freedom to consent or not… in this case, Mary readily said yes. The length of the betrothal was up to one year, with the marriage concluding earlier with the Rabbi's agreement.

The day was celebrated throughout the town as everyone knew Joseph bar Jacob and Mary ben Joachim… there was dancing and well-wishing as soon as the news spread. Joseph agreed that Mary should stay with her parents while he continued to work… he planned on giving her a ring of betrothal as soon as he could afford it. This getting to know one another within the context of family and chaperones continued for about one month at which time Mary's family got news of her cousin Elizabeth's pregnancy. They convened a larger family gathering to see who could go and assist, as was Jewish custom. Mary and two other women were finally chosen… and with Mary, Joseph was consulted and agreed.

The women would not travel alone as it was too a dangerous and lengthy journey. From Nazareth to Hebron, where Zacharias and Elizabeth lived, was south of Jerusalem… all totaled, about 100 miles from Nazareth. So Joachim paid for them all to travel by caravan to Jerusalem, and Zacharias would meet them with others, who would guide them, hopefully safely, to Hebron, and Elizabeth.

The trip was difficult, with unruly camels, a small robbery at the end of the caravan, and at night… but Mary and the other women arrived in Jerusalem as expected, and were escorted south to Hebron by a now mute Zacharias and several young men studying under him.

Elizabeth was anxiously awaiting her kinfolk, and was 6 months into her pregnancy when they finally arrived… first the men, then her 2 older cousins, and finally, at the end of the line, was Mary. Elizabeth, un-explicably, and at her condition and age, fell on her knees, and greeted Mary.

"Blessed *are* you among women, and blessed *is* the fruit of your womb! And how has it *happened* to me, that the mother of my Lord would come to me? For behold, when the sound of your greeting reached my ears, the baby leaped in my womb for joy. And blessed *is* she who believed that there would be a fulfillment of what had been spoken to her by the Lord."

Mary, bowing now, replied…

"My soul exalts the Lord, And my spirit has rejoiced in God my Savior. For He has had regard for the humble state of His bond slave; For behold, from this time on all generations will count me blessed. For the Mighty One has done great things for me; And holy is His name. And his mercy is upon generation after generation toward those who fear him. He has done mighty deeds with His arm; He has scattered *those who were* proud in the thoughts of their heart. He has brought down rulers from *their* thrones, and has exalted those who were humble. He has filled the hungry with good things; and sent away the rich empty-handed. He has given help to Israel His servant, in remembrance of His mercy, as He spoke to our fathers, to Abraham and his descendants forever."

The women embraced and were silent for a long time… something was moving between them… powerful, unseen. Elizabeth whispered, "I feel angels", and kissed Mary, tears running down her face… Mary, as she held her, answered, "Yes, they will always be with us… in joy, and in sorrow."

Mary stayed with Elizabeth and Zacharias until the child John was born… and hearing Zacharias speak his name was yet another confirmation of what had in fact happened to her, months ago on the roof in Nazareth. She herself was growing with child, and news had trickled back to her home town. Spending hours in prayer and service while in Hebron, her physical and spiritual peace drew visitors unexpectedly to her… word had spread that since Mary arrived, Elizabeth had grown stronger, healthier, as the birth drew near… women with child came to see… and seeing, wanted to touch Mary's garments, spend time with her she was so radiant… and some, even to kiss her feet. This was highly unusual in Judaism… and unprecedented in Hebron.

Back in Nazareth, the Rabbi and Elders of the synagogue had convened a meeting regarding the reports coming from Hebron… specifically, that Mary seemed to be with child. They agreed that consulting with Joseph was required before Mary returned… word had reached them that she in fact would be departing from Zacharias and Elizabeth as soon as the child was born, and all was well with mother and child… so there was an urgency to counsel Joseph. Upon agreeing, even as the Rabbi pensively held back his opinion… he was preoccupied somehow… remote… the Elders would recommend to Joseph that he carry out the marriage to Mary, thereby saving her family and herself Judaic disgrace… but at a proper moment, dissolve the marriage quietly. They would strongly encourage and support this action.

So two nights later, Joseph was asked to come to synagogue after his evening meal. They prayed and spoke wisely, given the situation. Joseph too had heard the news from Hebron… but he also remembered the white light which engulfed Mary on the roof, months ago… and, he had been dreaming… of angels… but he spoke none of this to the Elders. The Rabbi stood back, as if separated somehow from the judgment. Joseph nodded and thanked the Elders… but stayed behind as they trickled out and down to their homes.

"Rabbi… you have been unusually quiet, I would respectfully hear your counsel, if you will share it?" Rabbi Shmuel stepped forward, head down, hands clasped. "Joseph bar Jacob, my yoke is justice more than anything else, as you know… and I concur with the judgment of the Elders, ***if*** they are judging rightly, for we have seen this kind of thing before… but I must be honest, Joseph bar Jacob… I am not at all sure Mary is guilty of **any** un-pure action." Joseph stood up. He looked into the eyes of the Rabbi, now illuminated only by candles. "Nor am I, Rabbi." And he told him the story of what he saw on the roof, and the unusual fragrances in the air of Nazareth that day. The Rabbi remembered… falling asleep in moments, even though he was not tired… he could not explain it. "This news of Mary, who may be with child, so kind and devoted to her faith… has set something on fire in me since the news reached my ears." He walked to the scrolls and selected the one he loved most, Isaiah. He took it to the tabernacle and rolled it to 7:14… "Joseph, you know how I see Nazareth as the place of which the Branch from the Root of Jesse will spring, and the Spirit of the Lord will be upon Him?"

"Yes Rabbi", Joseph's heart was racing now.

"Well, there is another verse from Isaiah… 7:14" He bent over the scroll, taking time to put it together in his head… and heart. "Therefore the Lord himself will give you a sign: The virgin will conceive and give birth to a son, and will call him Immanuel." He looked up… "We must consider this, Joseph bar Jacob… especially when we identify Nazareth as the chosen place… we must also consider Mary as the chosen Virgin. Since the news entered these walls, I have thought of nothing else. Yahweh has a plan, I am sure of it… and we are part of that plan. We must trust this, Joseph… that is all I can say… I feel it in my heart. I pray that you feel it in yours."

Joseph pondered this. Here was a man, his Rabbi, whom he trusted and learned much from, counseling him to believe, as ***he*** now did, that the God of his fathers had chosen Mary to bear the child who would deliver His people. The prophecy was truly coming to pass… in **this** place, in **this** time.

Joseph rose and faced the Rabbi, hands outstretched, gripping the arms of the holy man… "I do feel it, Rabbi"… tears lining his face… "I have seen it." They embraced, and Joseph, his majestic frame, walked slowly down the hill.

"Praise be to Yahweh" prayed the Rabbi, "Praise His Holy Name."

That very night, the angel Gabriel appeared to Joseph in a dream and confirmed all that he and the Rabbi had thought and felt and even prayed about. Joseph awoke with an energy he had not felt, and a love he had never known.

He shared the events with the Rabbi as soon as he dressed and mounted the hill… "Mary is my wife, Rabbi, and always will be… and I will raise this holy child as my own… loving him, protecting him, laying down my life for him if that is what is needed". The Rabbi embraced him as he knelt before the Torah… "Joseph bar Jacob… He is coming… rejoice and be glad." And with that the Rabbi smiled and kissed him… and they fell on their knees in prayer.

At that exact moment, John bar Zechariah, later to be known as John the Baptist was born in Hebron. Zechariah, who had been struck mute in the temple at his lack of faith, immediately had his voice restored, and **this** did he prophesize:

> "Blessed be the Lord God of Israel, for He has visited His people, and raised up a horn of salvation for us in the house of His servant David, as He spoke by the mouth of His holy prophets from of old, that we

> should be saved from our enemies, and from the hand of all who hate us; to perform the mercy promised to our fathers, and to remember His holy covenant, the oath which He swore to our father Abraham, to grant us that we being delivered from the hand of our enemies, might serve Him without fear, in holiness and righteousness before Him all the days of our life. And you, child, will be called the prophet of the Most High; for you will go before the Lord to prepare His ways, to give knowledge of salvation to His people in the forgiveness of their sins, through the tender mercy of our God, when the day shall dawn upon us from on high to give light to those who sit in darkness and in the shadow of death, to guide our feet into the way of peace."
>
> **Luke 1:67-79**

Years, decades, later, Zachariah's words would be fulfilled as his own son, now known as John the Baptist, preached and baptized those repentant of their sins, and converting their hearts from Roman and pagan influences… he did this in the Jordan river, as it runs from the Sea of Galilee in the north, to the Dead Sea in the south.

> "And this is the testimony of John, when the Jews sent priests and Levites from Jerusalem to ask him, 'Who are you?' He

confessed, he did not deny, but confessed, 'I am not the Christ'. And they asked him, 'What then? Are you Elijah?' He said, 'I am not'.

'Are you a prophet?' And he answered, 'No'. They said to him then, 'Who are you? Let us have an answer for those who sent us. What do you say about yourself?' He said, 'I am the voice of one crying in the wilderness, Make straight the way of the Lord', as the prophet Isaiah said.' Now they had been sent from the Pharisees. They asked him, 'Then why are you baptizing, if you are neither the Christ, nor Elijah, nor the prophet?' John answered them, 'I baptize with water; but among you stands one whom you do not know, even he who comes after me, the thong of whose sandal I am not worthy to untie.' This took place in Bethany beyond the Jordan, where John was baptizing."

John 1: 19-28

The Road to Bethlehem

"In those days a decree went out from Caesar Augustus that all the world should be enrolled. This was the first enrollment, when Quirin'ius was governor of Syria... And all went to be enrolled, each to his own city. And Joseph also went up from Galilee, from the city of Nazareth, to Judea, to the city of David, which is called Bethlehem, to be enrolled with Mary his betrothed, who was with child."

Luke 2:1-6

Virtually all of Nazareth, those who needed to travel to their birth towns and cities, had already done so. Joseph, had spoken with the Roman Centurion who was in charge in Nazareth, was told that "there is a timetable which has been set to enroll... there are penalties if the people do not sign up in time." Mary was on her way back from Hebron now, but was heavy with child... so the journey would be a cautious and a slower one than usual. He had to be fully prepared, with a full day of rest for Mary at least, to leave for Bethlehem. His donkeys were strong and sure footed... Joseph was a kind man, who treated his animals very well... good food, clean water, clean stalls, and plenty of exercise without overdoing it. And his newly built seat for Mary, atop the strongest donkey, was specially fitted with sheepskin for softness, and fashioned, as only a carpenter could, with a riding handle, a back, also covered in sheepskin, and a small step to rest the feet for either side... allowing Mary to ride facing away from the sun or wind no matter which direction. The second donkey would be for provisions... which he had packed, and had ready. He now needed Mary to arrive and get sufficient rest before they began their journey. There was one other thing Joseph would be sure to know... if someone else from Nazareth would also be traveling toward their destination... for as he knew, there would be safety in numbers.

It was now the second day since Mary's return from Hebron. News of her condition with child was cascading through the town. Joseph and the Rabbi had put into motion a solution to preserve Mary's and her family's reputations... the Rabbi would marry them on the eve of the third day, quietly, in the synagogue. Only the closest members of each family were invited to attend...

All who were there were astonished by the stunning radiance of Mary... so simply dressed, yet so resplendent.

The Rabbi was unable to take his eyes off her... what he'd believed would be an anxious, quickly conducted ceremony, suddenly slowed with a growing peace, and even joy. It was all flowing, like the fragrances months ago… but this time, from Mary herself.

The Rabbi moved, as he had moved so many times before, lighting the candles, igniting the incense… but his state was almost dreamlike… as if the "shekinah", the Glory of the God of Israel was here… in this room.

The words were said… the law fulfilled… and when he had finished, the Rabbi did the extraordinary… he lay prostrate on the dirt floor… kissing the feet of Mary and Joseph as he did so. He was murmuring prayers into the soil where they stood. Then, after several minutes, he rose… and began singing… clapping as he went around the room… singing songs of praise to God. The families joined in. Joseph and Mary embraced… and the power from her womb went out to them all.

After a time, and a short meal in the room adjacent, the families embraced, bowed respectfully to Rabbi Shmuel, and left. Joseph, Mary, and the Rabbi were now alone as the Rabbi led them into the synagogue proper. He stood before them and took their hands in his.

"I have been told, in a dream, that we will not meet again in my lifetime" the tears now welling up and spilling down his cheeks… "I see great joy, but also great sorrow in the time you are yet to live… and this child, sent by the Ancient of Days to all of us, will change all things forever… this, Joseph bar Jacob and Mary ben Joachim, is the comfort I will dwell in every day… the promise of the prophets, fulfilled." And with that, he gave his blessing and went off to pray.

The next morning, as familiar as if they had been rising together for years, Mary and Joseph prayed, ate simply, and left quietly in the morning light. Mary, comfortably atop the strongest donkey which had been outfitted with a sheepskin seat with a support for the back… Joseph had initially made it, then changed and improved it to ease the difficulties for mother and child, as they traveled the long and dusty trek to Bethlehem. The second donkey was tethered to the first at a distance of about 2 meters.

Joseph was well prepared for this journey. Food, blankets, water, a document from the Rabbi, a money bag which he kept hidden on his person, a knife, and his imposingly thick and powerful red sandalwood staff. He had planned, if possible, to end the days travel near one of the many wells along the way… where they would stop, drink, water the donkeys, share news with other Jews, and then, move a short distance off, seeking a sheltered spot to spend the night.

And so they set out, leaving Nazareth, family and friends to register, as ordered, in the place of Josephs' birth.

At first, there were no fellow travelers… then, as the day wore on, the road became more crowded… with families moving, peeling off or entering at crossroads, singles or groups of men hurrying along toward Jerusalem, or just coming back… and intermixed with them all was a sound Joseph had never heard. Ever so faintly at first… a kind of hissing of the wind, but not the wind… at hearing it he turned, first this way, then that, but it was all around them… like the air itself.

"You hear it too then, Joseph my husband?"

"I do hear it, do you know what it is?... from where it comes?" Joseph stopped the donkeys. It suddenly grew very quiet… no one, now, was on the road, for as far as they both could see. "I have heard from the beginning…" said Mary. "What do you mean?... from the beginning?" Mary gazed deep into his kind and loving eyes… "ever since the Spirit entered me, giving Israel the Messiah." Joseph bowed and went to one knee. "Then you and the Child are a threat to the Evil One and his minions… the serpent… the unholy, the defiant One."

"Yes, Joseph… he is here… watching and waiting… letting us both know. Our strength is in the God of our Fathers… and, in you. For you have been chosen, my husband…"

Joseph stood up, kissed her hand, held his palm on her womb… "I understand."

Nazareth was far behind them now. They had descended into the Jezreel Valley where many lush and shady olive groves filled the land stopping several times to allow animals and family to rest and be refreshed.

But now it was the end of day, and the sun was beginning its daily journey into the sea… darkness would soon be upon them. Joseph searched for an outcropping, for protection from surprise from bandits, or anything else.

He found good sheltering for all of them just before a bend in the road… it was back, about 20 yards,

from the dust and noisy travel, and under an overhang of stone… a three sided stone shelter with a ceiling of solid rock. He prepared a place for Mary, helped her to it, and unburdened the donkeys, fed and watered them, tied them slackly to the sturdy trunk of a small tree. They were right beside the family, so all were within his easy reach if trouble started. He built a fire and prepared a meal.

Mary and Joseph prayed, thanking God for their marriage and His protection. Tired from the long day's journey, Mary, covered herself in sheepskin… kissed her husband, and fell fast asleep.

Joseph, gathered more wood for the fire, and perched himself beside her sitting up against the rock wall. He could see much from this position… and his staff lay between them, at the ready.

Soon, he too began to doze, head bobbing slightly as he drifted into a light sleep… it was pitch black, except for the remnant of fire which he quickly re-supplied, when he was jolted awake. The hissing had started again. As he gazed through the flames he could see strange, continually changing, dark shapes, like shadows, across the road, rising up from the ravine. They were cold, and menacing. His heart began to pound. He fingered his staff.

It was then, in his peripheral vision, off to his left, beyond the donkeys (who were quiet and nuzzled together), beyond the edge of the firelight, he saw a solitary figure. It was the figure, the angel that had come to him in his dream. The angel was massive, with huge arms and legs… wings folded down its back… there was a kind of glow coming from him. He kept his face turned toward the shapes rising and falling… but with one wave of his enormous hand, he motioned to Joseph to settle down and sleep… he spoke to Joseph in his mind… "sleep, Joseph bar Jacob, the Angel of the Lord will protect you all."

And with that, the angel stopped the hissing with another wave of his powerful hand…. sending Joseph into deep, restful, renewing, sleep.

Sometime in the pre-dawn hours, Joseph heard a rolling cart go by.... a man speaking to his donkey as they went. Joseph got up on his elbows to look around, and all was quiet. Mary slept soundly, warm under the sheepskin. Joseph laid back down thinking on all that had come to pass. Then closed his eyes.

They awoke with the sunrise… Joseph tending the animals, grooming them (which they loved) and readying them for the days' journey. Then, after feeding and watering, he loaded the provisions and the riding seat, and went to sit with Mary, who had prepared a light meal for them (more of it for Joseph of course, as he was walking)… then, after prayer and cleaning up, they moved back to the road and headed south.

Joseph had been following the tracks left by the cart and the man he had heard in the night… noted where they had stopped to rest, to refresh themselves (it was a good place, so they too stopped and rested), and that the man was walking, as he was, just ahead of his donkey.

It was mid-day when Joseph noticed a change in the pattern of the wheels… they began to zigzag, wildly… he stopped. Just ahead was a turn, with a boulder on one side the size of a house, and a ravine which dropped out of sight on the other. "A good place for an ambush by bandits", he thought to himself. He moved the knife closer to the front of his sash, his grip tightening on the thick, powerful staff. A few more steps, and the tracks of the man and the cart were gone… the ground was scuffed with dig marks and more footprints… many more, and what looked like blood near the edge of the ravine… only the donkeys tracks moved ahead… and he could see resistance in the donkeys hoof markings. He steadied himself… turned toward Mary.

"Mary, there might be trouble just ahead, I see unusual markings on the road… please hold on tightly."

And no sooner had he said this than four men, all smaller than Joseph emerged from behind the boulder.

They spread out and blocked the road… two on each side of the donkeys, who were beginning to get skittish.

The leader of the group spoke. "You travel alone on dangerous roads, my friends… no caravan of journeymen with you… why is that, may I ask?" The others started to move wider as he spoke, trying to form a circle around them.

"We go to the place of my birth, for the census." Joseph held the lead rope of the donkey Mary rode very tightly as he answered.

The leader laughed out loud… and pulled out a knife. "I do not think you will make it my friend"… and he rushed at Joseph. Letting go of the rope, Joseph thrust his staff into the midsection of the charging man, crumpling him to the ground… then in one motion, turned and swung the great stick at the second man behind him who was trying to cut the rope, separating the donkeys… Joseph struck the man's wrist breaking it cleanly, and brought the wooden weapon up to the man's chin, knocking him out.

Joseph leapt over the donkey swinging the mighty stick against the left knee of the third man, shattering it on contact. The fourth man began to turn and run, and Joseph swung at his ankles… crushing them both.

This was over in less than 90 seconds. All four men down, some conscious, the others howling in pain and cursing.

Joseph went close to Mary, who seemed strangely assured and calm in this mayhem… "are you and the Child, unhurt?" he asked.

"Yes Joseph, we are unhurt. God is with you my husband… there can be no doubt."

Joseph calmed the animals and repaired the rope after moving away from the injured men. He walked then to the ravine edge. Looking down a great distance, he saw bodies on the rocks, and several shattered carts. He stepped back.

He turned back to the men… "you have thrown these people to their deaths… I should do the same to you… whether you are Jews or not, you have broken our sacred law given to us by Moses from our God… you have murdered these people"… Joseph walked up to the leader still on the ground with a knife in his hand… Joseph drove the tip of his staff straight into the mans' hand… bones broke, the man screamed in pain… "we shall return this way, and I would not be here if I were you, when we do."

With that, he spat on the ground, and moved the two little donkeys along, cautiously, around the bend.

After several more hours, and a rest or two, it was time to scout for a place to spend the night. This place was more open than the last Joseph thought, but there were two trees, thick with growth. They would provide cover and were off the road a fair distance. He settled the animals in, fed them, watered and groomed them. They had performed well this day… he rubbed between and behind their ears, and they nuzzled for more.

He turned and found that Mary had built a good fire, and had gathered much wood… "Mary", he said coming up to her… "you are full of surprises." And he smiled at her.

"I have made the meal too, Joseph… please sit and eat."

And with that, they prayed and ate as darkness descended outside of the light of the fire. "Do you hear it?" asked Mary. "Not yet… no, wait, I do hear it… the strange hissing from beyond the road." He looked that way. "And the shadows have returned."

Joseph looked for the Angel… finally he saw him, closer to the road… sitting atop a large boulder. He turned to lock eyes with Joseph and nodded… then faced forward, keeping the shadows away.

The animals, Mary, the Child in her womb, and Joseph all slept soundly… the fire, mysteriously, burned all night… and the great stand-off at the edge of darkness continued… without their knowledge.

The next day was filled with people hurrying the main route to Jerusalem. The city, and especially the great temple could be seen for miles away… it was constructed, over time, on three large hills, with the temple being re-built by King Herod on Mount Moriah, the highest, and flattest of the three. The little train of Nazarenes mixed easily with the crowds as they continued on toward Bethlehem. Joseph had thought before the journey, that Mary would need more rest, more attention, as she carried her Child… but she amazed him with her stamina and resolve. They, by the grace of God, would reach Bethlehem by afternoon tomorrow.

Even with all the pilgrims and families, Joseph was warned by the Rabbi to be wary near the great temple, and the great city. Thieves and highwaymen and common criminals often robbed the unprotected, the unwary. They dressed and mixed easily in the moving throng… often working in twos and threes to create confusion and chaos while singling out a target. So, even while leading the animals, Joseph was always cautious of the situation… of the closest people. These criminals were not disgraced to push a pregnant woman from her donkey if it could get them what they wanted… so Joseph shared the Rabbi's words, and she held fast and tight to the handle Joseph had built into the seat.

As the time neared for finding a place to stay, Joseph counseled with Mary about where to stay… "I am not yet ready, Joseph, to give this Child to the world… we can sleep as we have been."

So he found them a quiet spot just off the road with several families and children, and exchanged greetings and prayers with them all. It was an uneventful night.

Joseph refilled the water bags early the next morning, feeding the donkeys and brushing them down. Mary rested and spoke quietly as other women came to visit her. "Yes" she said several times, "I think it is almost time." And smiled a gentle, loving smile as they took her hand. "Shalom" the women would say, and wander back to be with their families.

Joseph prepared breakfast as all this was happening… noticing also the traffic on the road, going both ways, was increasing. It would be the final day of their Bethlehem journey… for the census signing was an easy process, efficiently run by the Romans or their appointees.

The roads however, were so crowded as to be, in some places, completely un-navigable. There were no soldiers to keep the mass of humanity, so close to Jerusalem moving, so the roads clogged in both directions. Dust, heat, the yelling and cursing, animals being whipped, and bandits mixing and stealing and getting away… this was the temper of the day… and the pace was agonizingly slow. Joseph had to stop several times because Mary's discomfort was increasing.

Finally, nearing the middle of the afternoon, Joseph had come to the place of registration… there were several lines, and the Romans were keeping the animals away from the chaos. People were paying to move up in line so they would not have to wait.

Joseph, looking around, found a young boy, Ezra, who was selling loaves of bread with his brother. He led the animals to Ezra… "how much have you made selling your bread?" Ezra told him. "I will double it if you stand fast and hold our two donkeys. I need to register for the census, and my wife is with Child. Can you do this?" Ezra looked at Joseph, this massive man with his staff… he called his brother over. "Brother, take my loaves and keep selling… I am hired to hold these animals. The money is more than both of us have made, so I will do it." His brother took the loaves and went off.

"Thank you" Mary said. "You are eight or nine, no?"

"Yes, I am nine… my brother Enoch is eight." Joseph handed him the money surreptitiously… he did not want bandits to make the boy an easy target. Joseph stood up.

"I will give you more, if all goes well." And went to the middle line.

Ezra was gentle with the donkeys… giving them water, and brushing them down. "You are very kind… what is your name, may I ask" spoke Mary.

"It is Ezra, son of Eben… not too long I will make my bar mitzvah and be Ezra bar Eben."

"You are strong and gentle at the same time… a rare gift", said Mary. About 30 minutes had passed, and Joseph was next in line. He propped his staff against the table and got out his papers. It was now his turn.

The Roman looked at him. "Write your name and place of birth here" and pointed to a spot on the scroll. Joseph passed him the papers and signed his name. "Now write if you are married, single or have children." Joseph did that as well. "Mary, my wife" and he pointed to the donkeys off to the left, "and Yeshua, our little boy"… the Roman looked, Mary was turned away from him so he could not see her condition, Joseph began speaking to it, but never got to finish… because a multi-person fight broke out the next line over… the Roman looked back quickly, told Joseph to go, gave him his papers, and estimated Mary's age, and the age of the boy holding the animals, and wrote it down. He then left his post to help with the fight, sword drawn.

In addition to Joseph, the census read, Mary 20 yrs., Yeshua 6 yrs.

This census, which Herod himself would use later in his horror, mistakenly listed Joseph and Mary and Yeshua as an established family already… with no newborns.

Joseph returned and thanked Ezra, handing the same amount again… surreptitiously as before… so no one would see. He rubbed the boys head, and sought out proper accommodations, for Mary's time was near, at an Inn or House of Judah as they traveled south, near the edge of the city.

The Innkeeper

"Benjamin, can you believe this? The place is overflowing... everyone is ordering food and wine... we are making two years wages in just a few days. It is amazing is it not?" Benjamin, one of the innkeepers' sons could not even answer him above the din... so he just waved his hand and nodded. Aaron, the keepers other son was the cook, and he was a literal prisoner in the kitchen. "Do you sell food for the animals?" a voice boomed out from the crowd. "Yes" shouted Ephraim the innkeeper, into the air... "at my brothers place next door... he has everything stocked up for all the animals, whether they are burden beasts, or offerings... he has it all over there." And also added, "at the best prices in Bethlehem, too". Every room was crammed with individual travelers and families all mixed in together. The census requirements had become a boon for every business and street vendor in the town. Supplies were pouring in from the south along with people coming to log their names. It would never be the same here again. "Rome will swallow us whole" the innkeeper thought... but kept it to himself... spies for Rome were everywhere.

Insurrectionists found this time especially helpful as they could meet and discuss plans of all sorts as their response to occupation. Ephraim had listened intently at the bar and tables of the dining area… men were armed, and ready to ambush Romans and the soldiers of Herod when they got the chance. The day was late… evening breaking over the land. Men were crowded in the tavern area when a tall, darkly bearded, relatively young man, entered. He immediately garnered the attention of everyone. There was a presence about him. Something powerful. He moved easily through the crowd and came right up to Ephraim.

Then Ephraim woke up from his dream.

It was the same dream now for several months. True enough, the people were now beginning to come to Bethlehem, and also true, the rooms were beginning to fill throughout the town… but his dream was one which described a scene where the places were brimming with people. The roadways clogged and slow. This was the beginning of the great influx of Judeans… some of whom Ephraim had not seen for many years… and sadly, there were some who would not be coming back. But he was a businessman, his entire family was in the business of hospitality, and his brothers' family as well. They would care for the Israelites who needed a place, a meal, a time to rest their animals… whether they were passing through, or here to register because of their birth. The dream gave him insight, he believed, into what provisions the business would need to accommodate such a continued throng… he believed the dream was from Yahweh, "Care for my people, Ephraim". He heard this clearly in his mind. And sent out great portions of his business earnings to prepare. "We will be blessed" he thought... "blessed".

Ruth was Ephraim's wife. She was an honest and kind woman and mother... descended from the line of David. Ephraim also shared that distinction, and their wedding was a very happy affair... being good Jews, they knew the prophecies spoken of the Messiah. That he would come from the line of David, and strong references to Bethlehem even strengthened their hopes... maybe one of their own? Maybe the God of Moses and Elijah would find favor among them... or among their extended family? He would come from one of them, surely. They were attentive to the Mosaic Laws, they went to synagogue and the Jerusalem Temple at the prescribed times... they were good Jews, good parents. But as the years crept by, they got no sense from their sons that God had chosen one of them as The One... both slid into the family business and did quite well for themselves... Benjamin even becoming recently betrothed. So they watched, lived their lives, and waited with a kind of expectation... Ephraim even spoke to Ruth that he had a sense that something was about to happen...

The days passed, the roads became more and more crowded, the turnover at the inn was incredible... they had never been so busy... and the money was pouring into Ephraim's coffers. Business was, as in his dream, the best it had ever been.

But with the increase in business came an increase in strife... both within the family, and from without. The pressure to keep up with the demands which seemed to intensify by the hour drove the family into argument and accusation... Aaron needed help in the kitchen, Ephraim hired servants who were untrustworthy and made matters worse. The inn, where the family also had their rooms in the back seemed to be raucous all night... and on and on. They were all exhausted from the effort.

Then the criminals came in demanding money. This was a delicate situation as often these men were Roman soldiers dressed as civilians who, if not satisfied with the payoff, would be back in full battle dress to "question" the owner or his sons. Ephraim gave them as little as possible and much wine to try to sooth the situation. Fights broke out in the street when the Judean zealots suspected who was who. Ephraim did not need the full fist of Rome on his business.

And then he had this final dream. Everything was exactly as it had been before except that a voice told him to shelter the young bearded man and his wife heavy with child, away from the inn and any possible trouble... to give them privacy and quiet. Ruth was to bring clean linens to the place as a child was to be born there... a special child. The child Ephraim and all of Israel had been waiting for, for their deliverance. He was also told not to reveal this to anyone, but to make sure that it happened. Away from the tumult, away from the street thugs, protected and assured in safety.

Ephraim awoke at a very early hour. He prayed. He went out into the dawn to the place half hewn from the rock where sometimes he kept the few animals they had from the weather... but the animals were mostly in the fields now... he worked for hours cleaning and laying fresh hay and gathered stones and wood for a small fire. He brought clean water. Then went back to the inn and spoke to Ruth to bring the linens out. She looked at him. "You had another dream?"… "Yes" he said. "This one…" he was stopped by her…"was different" she said…"I know… they are coming here. I too had a dream. I will help Mary, that is her name, I will help Mary as she delivers. We are truly, truly blessed, Ephraim." And Ruth went out with fresh linens and herbs.

The day went like the mounting days before it except at the coming of the evening. Ephraim's heart was pounding in his chest as the minutes ticked by… then, as in his dream, a tall, darkly bearded, relatively young man entered the inn…. the effect was profound on everyone. He commanded the room as he easily moved through the throng over to the innkeeper… he leaned in to Ephraim, "We are needing lodging, my wife and myself, and our coming child… can you help?" The man's eyes were kind but strong… he was also a man who knew hard work as his forearms were powerful and well-muscled.

"Yes" Ephraim said, taking the man gently by the arm… "we have prepared a place". Joseph nodded and followed him. Ephraim left the inn, the strongbox full of coins, the clamoring customers, and everything else, and went outside. The woman was young. Beautiful as the early morning blossom is beautiful… and heavy with child. Ruth was already there. The woman, Mary, was riding astride a heavily padded donkey… the animal walked as if on a cloud… gently, surely. They led them to the half-cave which now had a small fire going… Aaron too had had a dream… he had come out early to start the fire and gather more wood.

"My name is Joseph" said the man, "and this is my wife, Mary… we have traveled from Nazareth to the place of my birth for the census... and it is her time to bring the child into the world..."

"We will give you all you need... and Ruth will stay and assist if you so wish it... she has done so many times for the women of Bethlehem"... Mary nodded as she moved from the donkey to the bedding Benjamin had brought out earlier... he was the only one of the family taking care of things back at the inn. It was all eerily quiet except for the soft crackling of the fire... then... as if from heaven itself, a great light shone down on the place. Ephraim fell on his face as did Ruth and Aaron... Joseph went to his knees.

For the birthing had begun. Soon, the shepherds and the angels would all be there, rejoicing, and praising, the newborn King.

The Shepherds

"And in that region there were shepherds out in the field, keeping watch over their flock by night. And an angel of the Lord appeared to them, and the Glory of the Lord shone around them, and they were filled with fear. And the angel said to them, 'Be not afraid; for behold, I bring you good news of great joy which will come to all the people; for to you is born this day in the city of David a Savior, who is Christ the Lord. And this will be a sign for you: you will find a baby wrapped in swaddling clothes and lying in a manger.' And suddenly there was with the angel a multitude of the heavenly host praising God and saying,

Glory to God in the highest, And on earth peace among men with whom He is pleased!"

Luke 2: 8-14

This is not an easy story to tell. It is full of personal hardship and near ruin... but ultimately, one of triumph from those long and painful days. The reason I say it is not easy is because the times have grown even more tense then they were. We are cautious. The Roman presence has increased. Their culture and taxes are intolerable. And Herod Antipas is even more of a snake than his father. But the cord which binds these times to that time years ago is strong. We sense the same imminence we did then. A birth of something. Powerful. From God. The Baptist has proclaimed it from the desert. We feel it in our hearts. It is the same feeling, the same sense of preparation.

It is not easy, and I am a little fearful. I am afraid of the consequences for me and my family should one of you betray this to Herod's henchmen. But it is a fear I have prayed about, for the burden is great to share with you the peace and joy which this has brought to our hearts and minds. And as I say, the same sense, the same anticipation, crackles in the mind as it did those thirty years ago.

We are shepherds. My father, grandfather, uncles, brothers, friends... all. Shepherds, their wives, their children, sheep, dogs and wolves. That is all that has ever been here in the high hills of Judea.

I was only 8 years old when our way of life almost came to an end. But, my grandfather, the elder and leader of our families, a man of great wisdom born of hardship and blessing, held us together. For months he and the others had been steadily losing sheep to a mysterious sickness... and then, the death knell of drought rang in the hills. I did not know fully yet, what drought was, but I could see the ravages on the land. The pastures and green rolling plains were burnt and scarred, streaked with dying brush and paling grass. Weeks and weeks in the high country and the flocks that had survived the sickness were losing their weight, their endurance. The ewes were not giving birth, and the food was drying up.

Grandfather had taken to walking among the diminishing numbers, praying and praising God for all the blessings He yet bestowed on him and all the families. It was not an opinion shared by many of the men, including, I'm afraid, my own father, who looked upon that time more as a curse, and said so.

"How?" he would rail to my grandfather, "can you remain calm when our livelihood is dying in the fields, stumbling and falling from weakness and sickness?... And you praise God. Have your eyes gone blind? Can you still think straight? We need to leave this place. We are dying here."

And he was right (or at least as far as everyone else felt).

The men were arguing over the smallest of things. There were fights. Families would go for days without speaking, threatening to leave. Tempers were short, food was dwindling, and there was fire and suspicion in the hearts and minds of many. It ***was*** as if a curse had fallen over this place, over our life. The drought was squeezing the nourishment from the hills, and the beauty and peacefulness was emptying out of our lives.

I think I should tell all of you that my fathers' frustrations had roots in more than just the drought and weakening flocks. They drove deep into the bondage that held us under Roman rule. The taxes, the soldiers, the spies among our own people, the new laws, the confusion and imprisonment of so many of our countrymen… and perhaps worst of all, Herod the First, a monster among men… with crimes against his own people too hideous to talk about. And those who did talk about it, those who spoke out against him, mysteriously disappeared.

And **all** of this amidst murmurs of deliverance threading through Israel.

My father was in pain, but it was pain for his people, his history, and a total sense of helplessness against the darkness over the land.

And we had always had our problems with the wolves, that was nothing new, but what was new and frightening were the creatures that stole into our hills at that time. Almost as if to finish us off for good. They came, no doubt, drawn by the smell of death. But these were not the wolves with whom we had struggled for years… Grandfather called them "demons with hair and teeth, strong as none before them were strong, cunning as an enemy is cunning, and as elusive as smoke"… they "hunt like shadows" he used to say.

It was their howling and mewling that I remember most. A sinister sound it was. Driving us down, breaking us.

Grandfather knew they would come. They were here not just for our sheep he said, they are here to take ***us***, one by one… monsters from Gehenna… from hell itself.

So you must see that we ***were*** breaking… our life, our land, our very spirits. We needed as we never had. All except grandfather. A rock of faith through it all. At peace somehow, like living in a vision. He would console us, minister strength and comfort, and he would pray. It was like he knew something…

Increasingly unable to sleep, but not from worry or anguish, he arose this particular evening and taking his staff, walked round our camp in the middle hours, the darkest time of night. He would tell us later of a warm and gentle wind fingering through his hair… "blowing even in my mind" as he stood gazing at the upper hills. This wind was different, he said. Not only could he feel it on the outside, on his face and body, but somehow, on the inside too. An indescribable thing, this wind. He closed his eyes and remembered the better times and smiles crossed his lips, he prayed for them again.

He stood there for a long time with his eyes closed, he did not remember how long, but he thought the sun had come up… that's how bright the light was. "White light" he called it… but when he opened his eyes, no sun, no light, just the dark… deep and full.

The dreams of an old man some said at the beginning. A man blinded by the fear of failure and ruin.

He said it was God answering his prayers. They said it was his age.

But soon it was father *and* grandfather… then the other men… then all of us… getting up in the middle of the night, not understanding it, not resisting it… sitting, as one, gazing into the hills as if waiting for something. And always, grandfather praying, and leading us in prayer.

What was the first of many remarkable things that happened in those hills was that wind… always warm, always gentle, seemingly blowing right at and through us, and always at **that** time… always in the night.

Then, as we arose for the wind, first days, and weeks passed… then something else happened. Grandfather told us he saw lights, like white torches, very high in the furthest peaks and rocks. The younger men with sharper eyes said it was his mind playing tricks… but soon they too saw them, then all of us. White lights, just as grandfather had said, dancing and fluttering high in the hills… stopping, coming together, rushing this way and that.

We were amazed.

And our God, the one to whom grandfather faithfully prayed brought forth as if out of nothing a great light in the heavens… and it grew and grew, filling the dark. Fewer and fewer of us slept at all… the white lights in the hills multiplied and soon there was the unmistakable sound of voices singing and praising.

And with the singing came renewal. It did not come completely at first, but in chosen places. The fields without rain burst in lush greens and the blooms of spring, those places most desolate, now radiant with carpets of life.

And where were the wolves? Those harbingers of death? They had taken to hiding since the lights came. They had stopped their killing.

We all knew now, even the most zealous and angry young men, that God was touching these hills. He was giving us something. Something we had needed. He was focusing our attention. Tuning our hearing.

And then, just like that, the white lights were everywhere, covering everything. We were witness to miracles where only weeks before death was all around us. New lambs were born, the wool to be shorn, we could not keep up. He was blessing us yes, but it was somewhere else He was calling us to. It was to Bethlehem. The little town in the valley was where our hearts were drawn. The great light settled there as if connected to it now, bursting in the sky.

And all one day it happened. The singing which had filled the night now rang from rock and tree, and like the wind, blew right through us. And it moved like wind, yet slow and with purpose down and over ledge and field, flowing from everywhere into the little town, then, and for all time to come, God's holy place.

The rest of the story you have heard. The birth, the hosts of heavenly lights blanketing the little town… how ***He*** was visited by angels, and by us, the shepherds. My grandfather knelt in praise and thanksgiving… ***he*** knew… he knew of the renewal this child would bring.

The reason I have brought this news to you about **our** desperations and faithlessness is to call the Lord to **your** healing too… as He came to ours… to call Him to whatever droughts or darkness there may be in **your** lives as there were in ours… to call upon His blessings to shower you and His love to keep you. For this child whom Herod sought and schemed to kill preaches now and heals in Galilee. Jesus of Nazareth, born in Bethlehem, 30 years today.

Simeon

Many years had come in Simeon's life at the time of his blessing. The decades had worn him thin… racked him with pain. Slightly bent over now, he moved cautiously, measuring his steps. Simeon worked the potters' wheel, creating those instruments of clay so useful and so needed. And when one of the many poor came in to his shop with a broken vessel, he always made a new one… and never charged them. He would not take advantage of those suffering from poverty or ever refuse them when in need. Never had he done this. Psalm 41, had a powerful effect on Simeon: "Blessed is he who has regard for the weak; the Lord delivers him in times of trouble. The Lord will protect him and preserve his life; he will bless him in the land and not surrender him to the desire of his foes." And he was a master potter now… with several apprentices working the larger pieces (as he could only give in to the pain for so long). But they all knew, even when he was not present, the poor will be provided for no matter what.

Simeon was never far from the God of Israel in his heart or mind… following all tenets of the Mosaic Law. Unlike many of his countrymen who seemed to flow back and forth between hostility for their "enslavement", and euphoria for their "coming" Savior. Simeon kept his counsel with the Word, and, as an island of peace it seemed, in the daily turmoil of life under Herod and Rome, he stood out.

Not a Pharisee or Levite, not a Sadducee or charlatan of salvation… he was a "righteous and devout" man patiently waiting for a sign… reading the Torah, finding strength in the Psalms of David and the prophecies of Isaiah… and watching the times… for they were ripe with expectation.

Because he was not a priest, he could only enter so far into the great Temple of Jerusalem… but as the years grew into decades, every time he went there (not as frequently now in his old age), his certainty increased. "Something will happen ***here***" he would say to himself, "something few will understand or even notice… but the God of Israel will do something here that has never before been done… of ***this*** I am certain".

He spent extra time in his town with the rabbi… learning, understanding, absorbing, asking important questions. They had become friends, the old rabbi and Simeon. And they would talk not only in synagogue, but in Simeons' shop or either of their homes.

"We have many prophecies of the Immanuel" the rabbi would say… "who knows the mind of God?... why does He enslave us again?... and give us an Edomite for a King?" (the rabbi spat on the ground and waved his hand in the air). "You, are a good man, Simeon… a man the God of Israel can see and observe. You do not hide under a rock somewhere. You are neither a man of bluster nor outrage… (the old rabbi took Simeon's hands in his own)… you are a man of peace, my friend… and I think the man God sends His people will ***be*** such a man to tell you the truth… I know what the rumors are… that the time is near… and we are oppressed. But when have we not been?" The rabbi did not seek an answer from Simeon, he simply spoke the truth as he saw it. "I have also seen the explosion of magicians and fools in these times… ah" (and sighed with another wave of his hand)

"God has called us to Himself, and when have we obeyed Him? When have all the people taken Him into their hearts and obeyed? eh?.. better men than I can answer that, but I do not see it… not in our history, not even now. We bridle at the Word… we do not soak in it, change in it, become alive in it. You, Simeon, you are one who does this. You have let the God of Israel change you. Truly as I stand before Yahweh I say you shall be rewarded. You have fixed yourself on God… and have lived a life worthy of Himself." They prayed together for a long time then. He brought a peace to the rabbi, as he did to the synagogue, to the ceremonies he attended… yes, Simeon was a man of peace… and deep wisdom. The rabbi thanked him once again for coming, and praying with him. "You challenge me to be a better man, Simeon", and blessed him upon leaving.

This was a trying time for the town. It seemed as if the entire population of Judea was on the move, with hundreds, even thousands passing different ways as they struggled to return to the places of their birth. The roads were clogged and deep ruts were forming. Heavy laden carts were drawn by camels and donkeys… entire families were travelling.

By edict, every man (and family) were to be registered and catalogued from the towns of their births. The scenes were chaotic and sometimes violent as roadways meant for single traffic now congested with three and four or more groupings at once… some heading east, some south, others moving west… the local inns and hospitality houses were overflowing with the mass of humanity. Simeon himself was hosting two of his relatives' families… one of six, the other of eleven… straining an already difficult situation. People were everywhere. Dust, heat, water shortages… all made what seemed like an occupiers' edict that more onerous. Yet strangely, amidst all this bad blood and near exodus-like conditions, Simeon remained remarkably calm and even-tempered… even his constant pain was abating a bit.

"He is coming", Simeon softly heard in his mind… barely noticeable at first, then more forcefully, more insistent. "Amidst all this, He will be here." The voice was not his own. It was unlike any voice he had ever heard. Indescribable. Resonant with power.

At first he thought everyone was hearing it, then he discovered it was no one but him. There were rumors, as always, in Israel, of the imminent arrival of their Deliverer, their Saviour, their King. God had promised to raise Him up from the "root of Jesse"… from the tribe of Judah, the line of David. He would come from among Simeon's kinsmen. The rabbi reminded him of this many times… "He will be one of us", and the rabbi would close his eyes and whisper, "yes, He will be one of us".

A long time ago, Simeon had asked for one thing in his life. He did not ask for freedom from oppression from the Romans or from Herod's unpredictable and unbearable rule. He did not ask to be spared any suffering or pain either…

but he ***did*** pray then, and constantly since, to be alive to witness the Immanuel before his death.

Now something was building inside him. Something distinct and unusual for him… a restlessness. He had virtually never known inner turmoil before. He wasn't sleeping well these past days. Herod's henchmen, all in black on black horses, were constantly on the move… as if looking for something… or someone. They would stop whole groups of people on the road and move in and out, pulling things from carts and taking bundles from women to examine them. The rabbi had heard of travelers, not Jews, but foreigners of great distinction, visiting Jerusalem, seeking a king… not Herod the King, but a "newborn king"…

Simeon's thoughts collided and careened… "Can this really be true? Can ***this*** be the time?... Is our Saviour, prophesied so many times, finally here?... now, among us?"

"Go to the Temple, Simeon"… exclaimed the now insistent voice… "Go and see the Salvation of the people"… there was nothing else said… not when to go, how long to stay… nothing… just "Go".

Simeon put essentials in his satchel… for offerings… a little for his sustenance, and his staff. He told the voyagers at his house he was going to Jerusalem… to the Temple… that he was being called there. "Please give this package to the rabbi… I will be back, God willing… but only the Holy One knows such things"… they looked at him in amazement. And then he left.

Simeon traveled south. Along the same dusty, rocky roads that those Judeans, coming from more northerly towns like Nazareth heading to the Holy City and beyond to fulfill the mandate of the Roman census. Simeon who had been in pain for some years because of a deteriorating bone condition, seemed to move as if "lifted by angels" he said later… on his 2 day trek to Jerusalem.

When he finally arrived, the city was alive with rumor and suspicion. What the rabbi had said was true. Herod ***had*** been visited by the wealthy foreigners asking him to bring them to the new king born under the Star they had been following. He dismissed them but asked to send word back when they found him… so he too could come and worship. What was amazing was that neither Herod nor his necromancers ever noticed or predicted the Star… there ***was*** no new star in the sky for them. And since that audience with Herod, the priests in the Temple were arguing about the existence and actual observation of the Star… some saw it, most did not. All Jerusalem was ablaze with confusion and disagreement.

Into this atmosphere entered Simeon, the devout and righteous man. He had not heard until now, of this Star, and could not claim, himself, to have seen it. But he believed it… he did not know why, but he believed. He listened to the shouting and fists raised because of what it might mean… the Temple was an enormous place… and it was filled with masses of worshiping Jews. He knew this place quite well from his visits over the years, and without hesitation, without foreknowledge, he headed for the Presentation entrance. A special place where parents would bring their newborn sons observing the Mosaic Law requiring a waiting period for the blessing and cleanliness of the mother. He stood there as if in a dream. He was not leaning to support his weight, he stood, for hours it seemed, without food or water or rest… abiding a building euphoria he did not understand, but did not resist. His spirit, despite the lamentations and desperations all around in the Temple courtyards, soared with anticipation.

A light came into his mind. A gentle, meaningful light."Simeon", the voice came into his mind again... "your salvation is at hand". All morning long there had been a steady procession of Jewish couples presenting their newborn sons to the Temple priests and making offerings... none of them seemed unusual in any way. Simeon watched, but stood like stone as they passed. The voice changed all that. Not only the voice, but the sick, lying and moaning everywhere, suddenly stopped. A warmth and quiet penetrated the place. Time itself seemed to stop. Something important was happening. Something profound... even miraculous.

He was here. Simeon could feel it.

The place was transformed. A peace, which even Simeon had never known, was now among them. The peace of the eternal. The peace of God.

He turned. A couple made their way forward. He knew their names. He did not know how. He just knew. Joseph... Mary... and, The One... the child, Yeshua. They had brought a presence no one had ever known before... and all were silent before it. Simeon reached out and touched the family, halting them as they passed. He reached for the child and immediately the voice spoke in his mind... "Behold, the salvation of the world, the blessing promised to the people, the Messiah".

Simeon broke down and wept... with the tears streaming down his face he whispered words, especially to Mary, which he did not understand as he spoke them... and gestured for them to go in. The child, The Holy One, never took His eyes off of Simeon the entire time... the two were joined together somehow. Simeon had a glimpse of the Eternal from the child, and greatly, quietly, glorified Him. Joseph and Mary were astonished, but, at Simeon's urging entered the sacred place of Presentation.

In the Judaic tradition, Mary in the Temple (because of her time of healing from childbirth) could not enter the place where the brit milah would be performed... the "covenant of circumcision"... it was a sacred part of the Temple, so Joseph was escorted in by a young Pharisee, Joseph of Arimathea, studying under the Elders of the Sanhedrin, to the mohel who would perform the ceremony. The mohel prayed for the child, and the father and mother, and performed the ritual. Joseph, the young Pharisee, could not take his eyes off the child, Yeshua... he could feel something, a stirring in his heart... he became lightheaded and suddenly reached out and held fast to a Temple column as dizziness began to overwhelm him. All the words and actions of the moment had gone eerily silent, consumed by a blinding, unearthly light... the Glory of God had returned, His shekinah had returned... and as he slowly collapsed, still fixed on the child, the words of the prophet Malachi rang in his ears... "And the Lord, whom you seek, will suddenly come to His temple". He took several deep breaths as he settled to the floor... the Psalms drifted soothingly into his mind, "be still (Joseph), and know that ***I Am God***"... he felt hands trying to help him, but he was overwhelmed, and slumped into a strange, abiding, sleep. He was lifted then, and brought out of the room of circumcision, attended to, and placed on pillows to rest.

One last thing remained for Simeon to do. He knew what it was before it happened. He opened his satchel and removed all the coins he had brought with him.

Always there were Temple guards... different from Herod's soldiers, but they acted if necessary, on behalf of the king... and they, like the soldiers of Herod, were not beneath accepting bribes, or in the case of Herod's men, extorting the people. Two of them, closest to the Presentation entrance were now being questioned, alerted perhaps, by a cadre of the King's soldiers, as they continued their constant searching.

He waited until the soldiers had left and approached the guards. He glanced back to see Joseph and Mary and Yeshua coming out. He moved quickly and extended large handfuls of coins, all of high currency... "I would be grateful to you both to let this poor family pass... to let them on their way..." The guards looked at each other, then at Simeon, then at the small family approaching. The moment was tense. Finally one of the guards said, "they look harmless enough"... "we were told to be on the lookout for royalty coming to the Temple, and report their whereabouts... nothing about common rabble. We will take your money... the family can go." Simeon praised God in his heart, and thanked the guards and headed out a different exit... but not without looking back one more time at the small, inconspicuous, Savior of the World.

Herod

My name is Gorga, and I have just been immersed by the Baptist. He continues to baptize hundreds in the Jordan for repentance for their sins. ***I*** have repented. I have much blood on my hands and heart... and have done terrible things in my life... there are events I could have stopped and didn't. I do not know if I can be forgiven by God, but I pray. I pray with everything that is in me. The Baptist says "make straight the way of the Lord"... and I know who he is talking to. He is speaking to me... to my life... and there is precious little time now.

This story goes back many years. To a time when Rome was just beginning to have great influence in this country. We were, make no mistake, an occupied land. Roman culture insinuated itself into as much of our life as possible. They had an agreement with the king... in fact, ***they*** had appointed the king... "King of the Jews" they called him. His name was Herod, son of Antipater (an Idumean)... it was a complicated affair, how Herod became king, but it does or did not matter... his family is firmly established as the royalty here now. That is where and when I began my long, and now regrettable, association with Herod and his family.

As a young man I worked in the quarry. I was big, muscular… very strong… and quick with my hands. One of Herods' buyers at the quarry spotted me and asked if I would consider soldiering. Herod needed a constant army, and he paid three times what I made working with the stone… so I said yes. I am a Judean, it is true, but at that time, I gave no time to God. So they trained me… and I became a formidable foe. I killed in battle for Herod. I even fought a top Roman warrior without weapons in a kind of friendly competition and beat him. Herod appointed me part of his inner court of soldiers… men sworn to protect the king and his family. Soldiers had a certain status, and the inner circle soldiers had **great** status. We had horses, quarters, women, all the food and drink we wanted. And the king was ambitious… once he had confirmation of Rome behind him, he taxed the people heavily (with severe punishments if not met), and he built lavish palaces in several places… but for some reason, he concentrated, for almost 10 years, on the re-building and expansion of the Temple in Jerusalem. The Temple had been partially destroyed in the years before he came to power… and he agreed, with the "blessings" of the chief priests, to mine and transport all the materials needed from Judea (where possible)… and give to Rome the "leftover" business… but paying off all those who required it. When it was finally finished, as it stands today, he had doubled the size of the place… fortified the walls, repaired the plunder from the Roman soldiers and greatly pleased the chief priests, bargaining a peace and agreement to stay out of each other's affairs.

Now Herod was a cruel and heartless ruler… I have many stories which would cause you great distress to hear… things which he ordered his soldiers and spies to do which greatly hurt the people… broke some of them, killed some of them. He did things and we did things which we will have to answer to God for.

The reason I am telling you about Herod is because something happened those many years ago… that's when I left him… at that time. I am an old man now. I did not believe I would get to see John the Baptist… but by God's providence and mercy, I did… and he preaches of someone greater… the Messiah. He says He is here… now… among us. If this is true, and the Baptist points to the desert… "He is there… preparing… fasting… being fired by God. When He comes back, Judea, indeed everything, will change. The Messiah is here… now… rejoice and be glad."

Ah, the mind wanders now in the twilight years… I was talking about Herod… and I must include his necromancers… snakes walking on two legs. He relied on them for guidance in many decisions he made…. many policies he formed. They would conjure up spirits and tell him what they advised. But everything began to crumble, when Rome called for a census. This was not of Herod's doing, and he quietly spoke against it… expecting great unrest throughout the country as a result. He claimed it was unnecessary and would surely cause trouble… and it did. The zealots attacked us many times, with soldiers wounded and killed… even the Romans suffered attacks. The census allowed zealots and criminals to take certain advantages. They robbed and looted travelers. Herod had a shrewd mind and could see this coming even without his advisors… so he doubled the guard details at certain locations, especially the treasury and the Temple in Jerusalem. The attacks dwindled. The zealots headed back to the hills. Herod was always nervous about Roman political perceptions negatively affecting his rule, and a disorderly region would bring reprisals from the local procurator at the very least… so he used an iron fist to keep order.

The Judean population hated Herod and his family. Herod was not their king, he was Rome's king of the Jews… Herod was an Edomite, descended from Esau, and not from the line of David and the tribe of Judah. The Jews rejected him as their leader but could do nothing about it… he had an army of soldiers, and behind them stood Rome. So there was nothing to be done.

All this changed, when, in the middle of the census, Herod accepted an audience with three travelling merchant/ astrologers from the east. They were heavily protected by thirty well-armed warriors or more. There was no question they possessed great wealth… and they startled Herod when they revealed that they sought the new king born under the rising celestial star. Herod listened intently, as did ***his*** astrologers and necromancers. He celebrated a great feast in their honor… and invited them back on their return journey, and that they might bring him word of the newborn so that he too might honor and worship. But they did not return… neither did the spies Herod sent out to shadow them. The spies were all killed by zealots who watched the palaces. So Herod was blind to what was happening. He was a cruel man, as I have said, and a distrustful man, a murderous ruler. He sent for the Temple priests and had his astrologers killed (as they could not predict the star or its possible destination). Herod's necromancers were an insult to the Temple priests, so they kept out of sight…

"So" said Herod with a wide sweeping motion of his hand to the priests, "tell me about this newborn king in my country." Those sent by the Temple were all priests, but none from the high council and they looked at each other in confusion. "What do you mean, oh Herod?" said the spokesman. "What I say" said the king, "or do you not know of the visitation of the astrologers to my palace?" "We know of it… and we know of their errand in this land… but we only have prophecy to point to" "Then speak of such prophecy to me… I am curious and anxious about it."

Then they consulted one another after withdrawing a short distance and returned. The chief spokesman had given way to a younger man, a Pharisee, a man named Nicodemus. "We have the prophets Isaiah and Micah speaking to such an issue as this… Isaiah speaks of the coming of The Immanuel, God is with us… and Micah points to Bethlehem as the birthplace of a ruler over Israel… He will stand and shepherd his flock in the strength of the Lord, in the majesty of the name of the Lord his God. And they will live securely, for then his greatness will reach to the ends of the earth. And he will be their peace." Herod was speechless. He was also very sick. His health had been deteriorating for quite some time, and he stood only with the help of a scepter. "I will think on these things you have said today…" and he dismissed them.

When the priests had departed, and the doors to the receiving chamber closed, Herod wheeled around in his black robes, crouching and hissing… "There will be **NO** Davidic king… I will deny these Jews their prize."

And he said it again, this time with growing malice and venom… "Neverrrrrr" he screamed. And beckoned for the necromancers, and they flew to him like flies to carrion. He spoke to them in whispers so we could not hear. One of them becoming pale and shaken by his words. They nodded, one after the other as he pointed to them. "Very well" he finally said. "I will wait for word from the travelers"… but the word did not come. He grew panicky and paranoid… becoming more like a trapped scorpion with each passing hour. Finally, the heinous poison in his mind exploded as he unleashed his deadly plan.

"Gorga" he hissed… "assemble your men… I have important work for them to do"… his face distorted into something unrecognizable and then he said it… "I want them dead… ***every*** male child in Bethlehem… 2 years old and younger… weaned or still suckling… their blood must run… spare none lest you yourself take their place" he slithered among us as he said it, looking into our faces, measuring us… satisfied his bidding would be done, he sent us out. "Give no warning… now ***go***".

Even the most vicious soldiers among us found this atrocity beyond comprehension… but Herod promised death to every one of us if we did not obey… so we went to the garrison and readied them. Men threw up and flatly refused… some even being from Bethlehem itself, or having family there… but in the end, Herod had his slaughter. And was satisfied that there would be no Savior, no Messiah, no King for the Jews from his land.

This horror was carried out by others, as I fled as soon as I left the palace. I left all weapons and clothing, all money and possessions, and became part of the moving mass of people in Judea.

After the great days of mourning which came after, I was far away north… beyond Herod's reach. Shortly after, the words reached my ears that Herod was dead. And one of his remaining sons was now king. So now you know. And I know, that Herod was a beast among men… beyond any boundary of virtue of any kind… a loathsome, repulsive ruler belonging to Moloch and no one else.

And now, I am old. Repentant. Living a simple life. But my dreams persist. What I could have done… but did not. But now I know that Herod did ***not*** succeed. The Immanuel lives. And all my life I have prayed that it was so… all my life. And now, God is With Us, God is With Us… rejoice, oh Israel, and be glad.

The Magi (Travelers from Persia)

"Word has come today of the death of our great friend, Balthazar. I will pray as is our way, for his memory and his family. I am now too old to travel as we once did… so I will send representatives to his family and burial site. Gaspar will certainly do the same. And while I am saddened by this news, the loss of a friend and scholar and holy man who convinced us, years ago, to travel so long and so far… and of all our many journeys together, he, Gaspar, and myself, Melchior... and our many companions… Balthazar was the keeper of recorded events… his many scrolls written and then copied. I am seeking now to find, in my library, shuffling now as I do, the scroll of ***that*** journey… the one so filled with things beyond explanation… with wonder, terror, and ultimately, joy… but I am rambling with the mind of an old man… please wait a moment while I find Balthazar's account."

Melchior was anxious to find the scroll, it had been in and out of his mind since the news from Judea, just days ago, of a Rabbi who performed miracles and whose name was Yeshua… he had asked many questions of the deliverer of this news… "how old is this Rabbi?"… "where is he from?"… and most especially, "what are his parents names?"

And now, this news of the death of Balthazar… all this seemed bound up together somehow… intertwined… like their healings so many years ago… but he would let Balthazar's words reveal these things… if only he could find the scroll.

He ***would*** find the scroll, but not until after he woke up from a short sleep… the events of this day and of the past few days taking their toll on his now fragile body.

Melchior awoke with a start… a long remembered dream having returned once again. He sat up slowly from his pillow filled place on the lush thick rug and reached for his water bag. As he was sipping, his nephew respectfully passed through the veils to his library… "Deepest respect, my uncle… when I came by earlier you were soundly sleeping… you sent for me?"

Melchior stopped to think. "Ah yes… Atash… I favor is what I ask… please sit." Atash found his favorite pillow, as he was a frequent and welcomed visitor, and waited.

"My great friend, Balthazar has passed from this plane, as you know, and I have sent respects and representatives… it is a sad day, a moving of my heart."

"Yes, uncle… Balthazar, may he rest peacefully, was a good friend to us all."

"Ahhh" Melchior, nodding his head, managed a slight smile of thanks.

"I need your help Atash in finding, and then re-reading Balthazar's record of our journey, so long ago, to find the newborn king of Judea. You, I think, have only heard whispers of the story… but it is powerful… unlike any other."

Atash, who was beginning to recline, sat up straight. His uncle had been on many journeys… for him to say this, was something special.

"Why?" asked Atash.

"You will see" replied Melchior as he went to the wall of scrolls. "They were in order, once"… he shook his head… "but everything is jumbled now… we will need to search."

"Balthazar has his name, and the journey name… which we all decided was, Star of the King… you will see this on the face of the rolled narrative."

They both searched for over an hour, for Melchior had many, many documents… but finally, as his uncle sat for a few moments, Atash finally found the chronicle.

And with that, a great commotion arose from outside. Atash went to the doorway to see his uncle's old friend Gaspar just climbing out of his lounging cart. He needed help now, as Melchior did, but greeted Atash mightily with kisses on both cheeks, as was custom, and a heartfelt hug.

Melchior too, entered the foyer… he broke into tears at seeing his longtime friend, They embraced, and kissed, and embraced again.

"You have heard the sad, sad news then?" Melchior asked Gaspar.

"Yes, it was shared with me last night, as we traveled here. I see it as both heartfelt loss, and some measure of fortune that I would be travelling here… at just this time." He paused, looked at them both… "you have heard of the news from Judea?"

Melchior nodded slightly… "I expect, because of the great distance, you might surely know more… come, let us sit and rest… might you take some drink?" Gaspar said he would… so Melchior saw to it.

Coming up behind, with several more camels, was Faraad… Gaspar's son, and a good friend of Atash. They embraced as he entered the house. Melchior too embraced Faraad, and kissed him on both cheeks… "welcome to our home, good Faraad"… and bowed slightly.

They shared stories of their friend Balthazar. They laughed, they cried, and they wondered. It was then, that Melchior mentioned the Star of the King scroll which he and Atash had searched for and found… and after resting, intended on re-reading, re-living, that journey long ago. They invited Gaspar and Faraad to join them… then they would share a feast with the entire house and all Gaspar's companions.

As they seated themselves on comfortable pillows on the lavish rug, Melchior bid Atash to read the scroll aloud to them… pausing where he needed, to drink deeply of the cooled water, from the small cistern, half-buried to retain it's refreshing quality.

And so he began.

"My name is Balthazar. A merchant of rare gems and precious herbs, a student of cultures, as my father and grandfather before me. We are a people outside the rule of Rome… but not outside its business and trade, and it continues to enrich our towns and cities. Our history is one of conquering and being conquered… to this day, war and threats of war as new rulers emerge in neighboring lands.

I have never relied on signs from the stars or necromancers with their snakes to make decisions for my business or my family. I have been taught well by my father and grandfather… and now I teach ***my*** son.

We can be fierce and hard, honed by centuries of sharp collisions with other peoples. But we can be also kind and patient amidst the terrors that besiege us… our women still preserve these gifts, teaching and reminding us.

In great measure, that is why I write this. For I have been reminded. Re-minded… made anew… reborn. Changed, simply and uncontrollably. And not only me, but ***all*** of us who met along that strange path to Israel.

It all began with dreams. Dreams have an important place in my culture… but these were of a kind I knew of no one else having had. Exchanges in the mind. I had encountered something of truth… a light and warmth bathing all of me, from the inside out. An unsurpassed peace."

Gaspar raised his hand and Atash stopped. Gaspar looked at Melchior.

"Remember, Melchior, when we first met?... three roads converging into one at the oasis? All arriving at the same time? It was as if it was meant to be, eh?"

Melchior nodded, "as if it were yesterday." They paused in silence… a tear running down Gaspar's cheek.

Atash waited for a signal to continue. Melchior nodded.

"It all began as difficulty sleeping, which I usually do not suffer from, many months ago. It caused me no harm, it was just a bit of restlessness when all else waned in the dark. Then it grew. Hour after hour, week after week. I sensed power in my chambers… felt unseasonably warm on the chilliest of nights. I would hear singing, gentle, like a breeze, from my terrace… soft, enchanting hymns and words taking form and melting away.

'He is coming' the voices in their melodies would say, 'Praise the Father, He is coming'.

Questions came into my mind: Who is coming, who is this He the singers keep praising? I asked among my servants and friends, business contacts and officials of the palace… no one had heard anything of what I was talking about… there were no births expected at the palace.

I have slept little in these weeks since then, yet, the energy I hold defies all that. I am robust, alert, excited, all things one would not expect.

And then I was ushered from my comfortable and spacious home, nearly a palace to rival the King's. Night after night they called me, these singers… finally, even by name… instructing me to leave and follow them. I could not see them, but I could hear them… sometimes hearing nothing else. So, with a small company of warriors, guides, cooks and men to tend the camels and donkeys we rode… we forsook our homes, led by voices in the night, and moved toward the west.

Days, then weeks passed, yet food and drink were plentiful… never have our camels moved with such grace and ease. An erratic beast, often turning on its driver, but not on this journey. It is as if a kind of peacefulness has settled over them.

Finally, as if destiny itself had brought us together, 2 other small, equally provisioned and protected, merchants and counselors to their Kings, converged by way of different roads… upon the oasis where we now rest. Their names are Melchior, and Gaspar. Men of learning, and business… both with a story not unlike my own… the sleeplessness, the voices singing, calling them by name… beckoning, insisting even, that they come.

And especially, as we discuss these things together, we are guided by the new celestial star. A thing so bright that the ants in the sand are visible at night.

None of us, not our warriors, our guides, are anything but joyful. We have barely met, yet distrust and suspicion have blown away with the wind. It is as if we have known each other as friends, for years and years… laughing, singing, breaking bread… and hardly anyone sleeps. No one understands. We move now at twice the speed and yet seem stronger. We are all amazed."

Gaspar raised his hand for Atash to break from his reading.

"I have water to get rid of… more common now that I am old."

"You know where the place of refreshment is, Gaspar, please… help yourself. And while you are gone, I will send for goat cheese and bread and dates." Melchior clapped his hands and a young man came in to fetch the light meal… "and a little more wine would do as well."

Melchior thanked him and dismissed him.

"Atash, you and Faraad eat and drink something too. Join us before we continue."

They both nodded and thanked him.

After the interlude, Melchior bid Atash continue… and picking up the scroll, continued where he left off.

“It took many, many weeks of following this thing in the night before ***it*** happened. We now know from the shepherds we have seen. All in our company felt an excitement, a climax to an anticipation as if a marriage of heaven and earth were taking place. The sky grew and shone as if a thousand stars had fallen. The singing echoed as from every blade of grass. The night air had cool nourishment to it, a gentle enriching mixture all comforted by the radiant body in the heavens. As we moved on this night we seemed to glide without touching, floating over crevasses and rock forms, moving our feet in free space.

We were told… all of us… in our minds that He was now born. We did not yet know whom He was, but we did know, finally.

For we have seen Him. This Son of God.”

Gaspar held his hand up again. “Do you not agree, Melchior, that Balthazar had a sweetness with the words?”

Melchior nodded… “he was one of a kind, Gaspar... it has been our fortune to have met and become friends.”

And with that, a tear ran down Melchior’s cheek which he wiped with the back of his now old hand.

Atash nodded and continued…

“We did not feel disappointment in those days that followed, nor urgency even. We felt hopeful, peaceful in our journey, and determined to complete it.

All the changes we have experienced have not yielded to time or bitterness... we all still walk as one. Brothers in a foreign land, congested with skirmishes from would be robbers sent squealing... and caravans of shrewd and thieving merchants. We are stronger now than we have ever been. And we are ***close***... we can sense it. As the fragrance of honeysuckle wisping on the breeze, we know we are near.

But we are being watched. Our scouts report pale horsemen, armed as from a garrison watching us from the hills, then slinking away into bouldered ravines.

As we approach a blind turn in the road, suddenly there is a sharpness in the air... a cold, penetrating wind. We stop. Arm ourselves. The sound of many horses pounding the ground reaches us as soldiers, many, many soldiers... out numbering us 5 to 1 at least. And yet, our warriors, the best in our lands have almost grown huge as they are met by these riders in black. The horsemen are anxious as they inquire as to our business. But it is clear that even with their great numbers, it is their blood that will run in the sand, not ours. They come from the King in these hills, a man named Herod... Gaspar knows of him, and has warned us of his treachery. He is a thief and a murderer.

We counsel with each other as we prepare to meet him on the next evening. The feast is lavish, and we are welcomed as 'friends'... but we feel his cunning and his lying tongue as he strokes us with vacant and deceptive assurances of 'good faith'.

We bid him farewell yet know his spies shall follow, but even ***his*** spies must sleep... and so his treachery fails him, and the onus of the dark we felt flees us, as on the wind which it came.

Our hearts quicken as we climb into the high hills of lush green and treacherous rock. A contrast of peace and difficulty side by side. We are met by shepherds. People who tell us of a birth some days ago, and that they've been waiting for us. ***Waiting for us***. And they were singing. The same words, the same melodies which we have heard along our journey… it is as if the hills themselves were resounding with this music. They also spoke of frequent visitations. Angels they say come here… (we have heard of angels)… singing and rejoicing amidst their flocks. Their sheep have never grown so fat, so full of wool, they say.

These shepherds say also they know why we have come, and bid us their peace as they direct us toward a tavern in this little town we overlook, this Bethlehem."

Gaspar held up his hand, laughing… "do you remember, Melchior, how fat the sheep?... how full of wool?

Just astonishing to see such abundance." That's all Gaspar had to say, but he continued to laugh from his memories.

Atash took a small drink of water from the skin.

"It was dark when we arrived at the tavern. Someone going in must have spoken to the owner of so large a company just outside. We waited. But we did not wait long. The innkeeper and tavern owner, a man named Ephraim came out and took us to a small hill with an outcropping hewn out of stone. He gestured with his arms to this place. There were three of them, he said, with two donkeys. Joseph, of whom I had dreamt, Mary, heavy with child, and finally Yeshua himself. The child was born here because we had no room for them at the inn, he told us. The town was flooded with census pilgrims from all over.

Despite all this, all of his family, had dreams of this birth… and in THIS place. They knew that something important was to happen here… and it did. He told us of the shepherds, the singing, the women helping… angels in the hills. We look at each other, amazed.

And then he said Joseph and Mary took the Child to the Temple in Jerusalem at the appointed time for the ritual of brit milah.

They returned this way just yesterday… as they are heading south. We gave them a tent with poles… the finest my brother had… even a canvas floor to keep the scorpions out. If you are seeking them in peace, as I know you are, then follow this road south until you spot the tent and two donkeys. You will find them there.

We asked if we could spread out on his land for one night and leave in the morning. Ephraim was delighted,

and brought out much food and good drink for us and our men. All exchanged stories and histories until the day overcame us. We slept like babies.

It was two full days heading south and east following the trade route the innkeeper had pointed out toward the land of Egypt, before the caravan came in sight of the solitary tent and two donkeys. Night had just begun to swallow the desert. A small fire was just to the left, and downwind. We saw no one as we approached. The body in the sky had stopped directly over this place where we were. Our hearts began racing with anticipation and wonder.

Suddenly, a man, as big as any warrior came forth from the tent. Tall, sinews heavy and marked with enormous strength… yet, he had no manner of fierceness about him…

a quiet assurance as he calculated our number and met our gaze. He stood as if guarding the little tent, and spoke no words.

Finally, Melchior, sitting his camel down, came up to him and bowed… 'You must be Joseph', and bowed again. 'My name is Melchior, these are my friends, Gaspar and Balthazar… and our entourage. We have been on the road from distant lands for many weeks. We follow the celestial body' he gestured to it… 'a sign that something is changing in the world, a birth as important as a King perhaps… and we have brought gifts.'

At that moment, a woman emerged from the tent holding an infant. She was beauty without need of adornment… without need of spectacle or veil. A beauty as beauty can only be, simple, delicate, gentle.

'And you are Mary, are you not?' She bowed her head.

Melchior turned to his friends, 'our quest is over, we have found the one foretold by the star'. We all dismounted.

It was this couple, this Child we had come so far to see… and the singing, which was like wind in the background, grew louder… the words were the same,

'He is the Son, Praise the Father, He has come'… but ***who*** was singing this we did ***not*** know.

Mary came up to us… and pulled back the coverings. Only weeks old now, but wide-eyed and expressive… studying our faces. He spoke to us… not in words of course, but in our minds as he met our eyes each in turn. This little child gave to us reservoirs of solace and peace. It was now, at this moment, that life began anew.

We brought ***our*** gifts: gold, frankincense and I brought myrrh… the most that is precious in my kingdom. To heal, to clean, restore and encourage life. They graciously accepted our offerings… and in an extraordinary act of kindness, asked that each and every member of our caravan come and touch the hand of the little King… which they did. She spoke his name to each and every one, 'Yeshua is his name'.

We praised and hugged both Mary and Joseph, and blessed little Yeshua with the prayers of our people, and departed… returning by another way.

Filled with peace and wonder, changed by understanding, we all are re-minded. Made anew. Reborn somehow. Simply, uncontrollably."

Balthazar

When Atash concluded the scroll-reading, Gaspar, standing with some difficulty, spoke to him and Faraad.

"Both of you must contact Balthazar's son and put together a journey to Judea… I hear many things about a miracle-worker named Yeshua, the carpenters' son… he preaches and the crowds are spellbound… he has even brought a child back from the dead. I believe it is the same Yeshua, come now into public manhood as is the Jewish custom. Those many years ago, when we found the young family, we had a cart pulled by donkeys which was breaking apart… no one in our company could fix it. But Joseph did. He was a master carpenter.

You must now go, as we did, and find this fully grown Yeshua… and return to us with your own story."

Atash and Faraad nodded… they would go.

Printed in the United States
By Bookmasters